Hannah
in the Spotlight

'Full of fun literary and movie references and packed with family secrets and friendship dramas, this smart, charming book is perfect for Judi Curtin or Cathy Cassidy fans. I loved it!'

Sarah Webb, author of the *Songbird Café Girls* and *Ask Amy Green* series.

When Natasha was young her absolute favourite thing was reading everything she could get her hands on. Her second favourite thing was persuading her sister, brothers and neighbours to sing, dance and act with her in different shows that they performed for their parents and anyone else who would watch. Natasha loved her speech and drama classes (way more than school) and studied it right up to diploma level, taking part in various musicals and pantomimes along the way. One of her favourite books was *Ballet Shoes*, and she has read it so many times her copy is almost falling apart. As Natasha's siblings are now too old to be made take part in performances, she decided to create Star Club instead, and she is really enjoying writing about the kind of club she would have loved to join herself.

Also by this author, *Missing Ellen*.

Natasha Mac a'Bháird

Hannah in the Spotlight

STAR CLUB

THE O'BRIEN PRESS
DUBLIN

First published 2016 by
The O'Brien Press Ltd,
12 Terenure Road East, Rathgar,
Dublin 6, D06 HD27 Ireland.
Tel: +353 1 4923333; Fax: +353 1 4922777

E-mail: books@obrien.ie.

Website: www.obrien.ie

ISBN: 978-1-84717-845-9

7 6 5 4 3 2 1

20 19 18 17 16

Printed and bound by Nørhaven A/S, Denmark.

The paper in this book is produced using pulp from managed forests.

Published in
DUBLIN
UNESCO
City of Literature

Dedication

To Rachel and Sarah, who read it first.

Acknowledgements

A huge thank you to all those who read *Hannah in the Spotlight* and gave me their great suggestions – my young readers, Rachel, Sarah, Alice and Amelia, my one-time drama teacher and now friend Margot Keegan, and my mother Anne, who has always been my biggest supporter. Thank you to my book club friends for all your encouragement and for coming up with the title for me. Thank you to all the fantastic team at The O'Brien Press and especially to my wonderful editor Helen Carr – it is an absolute pleasure working with you and I'm so glad to have you bringing your talents and insight to my books.

Chapter One

It's impossible to get any peace in my house.

Either Zach and Bobby are chasing each other (or Maisie) around the house, or they're playing football on the landing and using my bedroom door as the goal. Or else it's Maisie taking over the sitting room with all her dolls and teddies, or Emma crawling along and wrecking Maisie's game. And then Maisie crying and having to be comforted, and Emma either laughing or else joining in and crying too.

I share a room with Maisie, so I can't even escape up there for a bit of quiet, because she's sure to come in and out getting more teddies, or wanting me to play with her. I have been BEGGING Mum to change things around so I can have my own bedroom, but so far the most she has said is 'we'll see'. Which is better than an outright 'no', but not by much.

I said it to Mum. I said, 'It's impossible to get any peace in this house.'

Well, you would swear I had just made the best joke in the history of the earth. She practically fell off her chair laughing.

'What's so funny?' I demanded.

When she finally stopped laughing enough to answer me, all she would say was, 'I've been saying the same thing for years.'

Which wasn't much help to me.

So there I was, the poor unfortunate eldest child, with four younger siblings causing endless chaos, and one unsympathetic mother who could only laugh at me. The summer holidays were stretching out before me, long and empty and very, very noisy.

I *really* wished I was going to drama camp with Isabel, a girl in my class. She'd been telling me all about it and it sounded amazing. The kids were going to write their own show and then at the end of the two weeks they'd put it on for their parents. Lucky Isabel – it sounded like so much fun. I would have loved every minute.

I didn't even ask Mum if I could go because it wouldn't have been fair. The camp was so far away – at least half an hour's drive. I couldn't ask Mum to load all the kids into the car and drive me there every morning, and then do the same again to collect me. Anyway, I'd feel a bit like I was abandoning her. Dad works long hours, and since Emma came along Mum has been relying on me a lot to help out. Even though Zach's only three years younger than me he's a bit of a daydreamer – he's got his head in the clouds most of the time. If you ask him to help with something he will, but I just do stuff without being asked. My brothers think I'm bossy, but actually I'm just pretty organised.

What I needed was a project. Not a school project, obviously. I'm not that crazy. The best thing about the summer is having a very long break from schoolwork of any kind. But I'm the sort of person who always likes to be doing something. I like to have a plan to focus on and to feel like I'm achieving something. I just needed to work out what that something should be.

The day before, I'd spent most of the afternoon playing teddies with Maisie. If I didn't find something to do quickly, I'd be sucked into another game. It wouldn't be so bad if I could call for Ruby, but she was at ballet camp that morning.

As if she knew what I was thinking, Mum said, 'Why don't you call for Ruby?'

'I can't, she's got ballet camp,' I reminded her. 'She's not going to be home until lunchtime.'

'Oh, that's a pity.'

I knew what was coming next. I just knew it.

'Why don't you call for the girl next door then?' Mum went on. 'She seemed really friendly.'

I'm not sure how Mum had worked THAT one out. The day before, we'd seen some new people moving in next door – a mum and a girl about my age. Mum kept saying she should go over and introduce herself, but something kept getting in the way, so all she had managed to do was say 'hello' as she rushed to pick Maisie up after she fell off her bike. They were unpacking lots of bags from their car at the time, and looked pretty busy themselves, so I don't really know how Mum could have somehow decided that the girl was really friendly. She might be lovely, sure. She might also be boring, or weird, or mean. It was a bit hard to tell from one 'hi'. But trust Mum to think that just because we lived next door to each other we were bound to end up as best buddies.

'She said hello, that's all. And only after you'd said it to her first.'

'Well, I thought she seemed nice,' Mum said. 'Anyway, why don't you call for her and find out?'

'I don't know, Mum. It's not like I'm Maisie's age where you can just go and play with anyone.' It was an important point, I thought. At twelve, you're a bit more discerning about who you hang around with.

'Come on, Hannah, it's the nice thing to do. She probably doesn't know anyone here yet. Why don't you see if she wants to go rollerblading?'

I could see Mum wasn't going to let the subject drop. And now that she'd played the 'nice thing to do' card I was stuck. 'Oh, all right then! But can you come and call me after half an hour? Then I have an excuse to leave if I've had enough.'

Mum laughed. 'No problem. I'll be sure to pop out in between feeding Emma and hanging out my third load of washing.'

'Hey, it's the least you can do after making me go off with a complete stranger,' I told her.

'You know what they say, Hannah. A stranger is a friend you haven't yet met!'

A stranger is a friend you haven't yet met? Yeah, right! Only the other day she was warning me about not talking to strangers, and never getting into a car with someone you don't know, even if they say they just want you to show them something on a map, and never going off with some-one even if they ask you to help them find their lost cat.

Although, to be fair, the girl next door didn't exactly look like the kind of stranger who would bundle you into a car and kidnap you. But you never know.

I went to the cupboard under the stairs to look for my rollerblades. Not an easy job, considering it's the place where all seven members of my family dump everything that doesn't have a home. (Well, I guess Emma doesn't, but that's because she's only eight months old. There's still stuff belonging to her in there, or things that used to belong to Maisie and that Mum is waiting for Emma to grow into.) Sometimes when we're having people over Mum runs around the house with a laundry basket and picks up all the clutter and shoves the whole lot under the stairs to deal with later. I've lost many pieces of valuable artwork that way; Mum just says that it's my own fault for leaving it lying around.

I opened the door very carefully, because you really never know what's going to land on top of you. Luckily I spotted my rollerblades right away, tucked under Zach's old tricycle and a pile of newspapers Dad claimed he was going to get around to reading at the weekend. I hauled them out, managing not to dislodge the entire mound of things around it. It took me another few minutes to find my helmet and knee and elbow pads, which Mum won't let me skate without, even though I pretty much never fall over.

'Hannah, are you coming to play teddies?' Maisie demanded. She was standing behind me, and as I turned all I could see was the top of her hair above her armful of stuffed toys.

'Not right now,' I told her.

'Oh, please, Hannah?' A blue rabbit fell out of the pile, revealing a sad little face.

I felt bad, but I needed some twelve-year-old company, even if it was the stranger next door. 'Sorry, Maisie. I'm going out rollerblading. Maybe later, OK?'

I picked up the rollerblades and headed for the door,

ignoring Maisie's protests. 'Bye, Mum!' I called.

Once I was outside though, I suddenly found myself feeling a bit shy. If you knew me you'd realise this is unusual. I'm sort of a leader in my little group of friends. I think it comes from being the oldest of a big family. You just have to be ready to take charge if you want anything to get done. So I'm not usually shy, but suddenly the idea of walking up to the house next door and introducing myself to these strangers seemed a bit daunting. I decide to go for a bit of a skate first, just to get into the right frame of mind.

I sat down on the footpath to put my rollerblades on. A gang of kids were playing football on the green, and some younger kids were cycling around on bikes and tricycles. Woodland Green is a pretty nice place to live, I have to admit. It's nice to have lots of kids around and a place to hang out where our parents aren't freaking out about us getting knocked down or something. Just a pity for me that the only girl my age is Ruby and her schedule is so busy we don't get as much hang-out time as we'd like. Well, there's also Tracey, but I don't count her. Tracey is the meanest girl I have ever met in my life. Her favourite thing to do is laugh at other people. She makes an actual hobby out of it. Unfortunately for me, she lives just two doors down from me, on the other side of the rented house. Just my luck that the nearest one of my classmates has to be meanie beanie Tracey.

I set off skating around the green, dodging out of the way of the little kids. It would be so nice to have someone new to hang out with. And having her right next door — what could be better? It would be somewhere to escape to when I'd had enough of my crazy family. I deliberately skated over and back in front of my own house and next door's. I was kind of hoping the new girl would see me, and she'd just come out herself, saving me the trouble of having to go and knock and introduce myself to her mum and all that.

'All OK there, Hannah?' It was Mum calling from the front door, Emma balanced on her hip.

'Yes. Fine,' I shouted back, hoping she'd just go away.

'Isn't there anyone home?' she roared.

'I don't know! I'm just going to see,' I hissed back, glancing around to see if anyone was watching.

Luckily shouts from inside our house told Mum that there was a fight that needed to be broken up, and she rushed off. I decided I'd really better just get it over and done with before she came out again. Building up speed, I went up the path once more, then whizzed around and back down, not slowing down as I turned the corner into next door's driveway. Suddenly their house was rushing up to meet me. I put out my hands to stop myself from crashing into their front door. At that exact second the door started to open and I fell headlong into their hallway.

Chapter Two

'OW!' I didn't know which bit of me hurt most. It was a close contest between my wrist, which had bent awkwardly as I tried to break my fall, my left knee, which had taken most of my weight when it hit the wooden floor in the hallway, or my right shin, which I had whacked on the step as I fell. *So much for all my safety gear,* I thought.

'Is that how you always come into people's houses?'

I looked up to see the girl next door grinning down at me. 'I was just going to come out and see if you wanted to skate together, but now I think maybe you're a bit of a liability.'

'It's not funny,' I muttered, rubbing my knee underneath my knee pad, which might have saved me from breaking any bones, but definitely hadn't stopped it from hurting. 'What did you go and open the door like that for?'

'Sorry,' she said, not sounding like she meant it a bit. 'I wasn't exactly expecting you to come crashing through it.'

I sat back and looked up at her properly. She had long blonde hair hanging loose down her back. She was wearing skinny jeans and a long T-shirt that said 'MEH' in really big letters. She smiled at me suddenly, and her smile lit up her whole face. I couldn't help smiling back.

'I'm Hannah,' I told her, getting to my feet, or rather my blades. 'Sorry about that. It wasn't exactly how I was planning to introduce myself.'

'That's OK,' she said. 'I'm Meg. So, do you want to go skating together, or do you need to take a break?'

I was feeling slightly bruised, but I didn't want to admit it. 'I'm fine. Do you have rollerblades, then?'

'Yes, but I'm not exactly sure where. Do you want to come in for a minute while I look?'

'Sure.'

I followed her down the hall. It's always funny to see our house in reverse. From the outside Meg's and my house looked exactly the same, only the opposite way around. Our sitting room window was on the right of the front door and that bit of the house joined on to Meg's, and the garage was on the left. Meg's sitting room window was on the left and the garage was on the right. The fronts of the houses were like mirror images of each other.

The insides were completely different though. Meg's house was painted cream all over – no, not cream – what's that really sensible plain colour rented houses always are? Oh yes, magnolia of course. The walls were bare, and the rooms seemed so empty, apart from all the boxes I mean

– there were no books on the shelves yet, or ornaments on the mantelpiece, or anything that made it look like it actually belonged to them.

Meg led the way into the family room at the back of the house. Almost the entire floor space was taken up with boxes and bags.

'I think I know what box they're in,' Meg said. 'Mum didn't want me to bring them because they're so bulky and take up so much space, but I knew I'd use them so I talked her into it.' She ripped the tape from the top of a box and peered inside. 'Huh – all her tennis stuff! She had room for that all right!' She held up two tennis rackets and a big sports bag, dumped them on the floor and dived into the box again. 'All her shoes too. And she thinks I have too many!' Several pairs of high heels came flying out to land on top of the tennis gear on the floor.

I was trying to work out her accent as she talked. She was Irish all right, but there was a hint of something else there too, I just couldn't figure it out.

'Aha!' Meg lifted out her rollerblades with a triumphant grin. 'I knew they were here somewhere. And here are all my knee pads and elbow pads and things. Mum insists on me wearing them – I suppose yours is the same?'

'Oh, yeah,' I said. 'She's very big on knee pads, elbow pads, helmets, seatbelts – all that stuff. I think it's some kind of a mum law that they have to be obsessed with safety.'

Meg was sitting on the floor pulling on her rollerblades. I suddenly realised how quiet the house was. 'Where is your mum, anyway?'

'Oh, she's gone out for the day. I've got the house to myself. It was starting to feel just a teeny bit too quiet, actually.'

'Oh my God, you're so lucky!' I told her. 'My house has never been quiet for a minute, ever. I can't actually imagine what it would be like to be the only one at home.'

'Really?'

I explained about all my siblings. Meg's eyes widened.

'Wow, you're the lucky one!' she said. 'I'm an only child. I always wished I had at least one sister to play with.'

I felt a bit bad. I knew I was lucky, really. 'Oh, I do like having a big family,' I said quickly. 'But sometimes I feel like I'd do anything to get five minutes' peace. I even have to come out to the front garden if I want to read my book because the boys have turned the back garden into a football pitch.'

Meg finished putting on all her gear, and we skated slowly to the front door. Normally Mum doesn't let me wear my rollerblades inside. But there were no grown-ups around to warn us about the wooden floor getting marked, so I glided along, enjoying the smooth feel of it underneath the blades.

'Oh,' Meg said, stopping so suddenly that I almost

crashed into her. I grabbed onto the banister instead. One crash in their hallway was more than enough for one day. 'What time is it? Sadie is supposed to be coming over to check on me at lunchtime.'

'Don't worry, it's only eleven. Who's Sadie?'

'She's my granny. I call her Sadie because Granny doesn't seem to suit her! That's OK then, I've got ages.'

We skated down the drive and started doing slow laps of the green. It was a bit quieter now – must have been snack time for the little kids – so it was easier to get around.

'So where did you used to live?' I asked her.

'Oh, we move around a lot,' Meg said vaguely. 'How about you – have you always lived in Carrickbeg?'

'Yes, my whole life,' I said. 'And your house has always been rented out, so we've had tons of different neighbours. The last lot were a big group of students, and they were really noisy. Mum was so glad when they moved.'

'Well, she needn't worry about us!' Meg said. 'It's just me and Mum, and we're pretty quiet.'

'What made you move to Carrickbeg?'

'Mum grew up here. She moved away when she went to college. My granny and grandad still live here, so Mum wanted to be near them when, um ...' She hesitated, then quickly said, 'when she decided to move. We used to come here a lot for holidays, but it's a few years now since we've been back. Sadie is so happy to have us near.'

'So is Meg short for Megan then?' I asked her.

Meg made a face. 'I wish! My real name is Margaret, after my aunt. But if you EVER tell anyone ...'

I laughed. 'I won't! Meg is much nicer. Makes me think of *Little Women.*'

'Oh, I love *Little Women*!' Meg said. 'Although I think I like Amy better than Meg. I always think Amy is a bit more real – Meg's just too good to be true sometimes!'

'Laura's favourite is Jo,' I said. 'She wants to be a writer some day, so she just loves reading about Jo and how she keeps on writing stories and trying to get them published. Laura's one of my best friends,' I added in explanation.

'Does she live on the green too?' Meg asked.

'No, she's a bit further away. Ruby lives just over there,' I added, pointing to Ruby's house about ten doors down from Meg's, and on a bend so that it was facing the green from a different angle. 'But we can't call for her.' I explained about ballet camp.

'Are you going to any camps?' Meg asked.

'No.' I sighed. 'I'd have loved to go to drama.'

'Oh, do you like acting?'

'I love it. It's my favourite thing in school – I just wish we could do it more often. Did you do much in your old school?'

'A bit. I love it too,' Meg said. 'That feeling of trans-forming yourself into someone else, getting right inside their mind and the way they speak and move.'

'Exactly!' I beamed at her. It was so great to meet someone who understood just how I felt about acting.

By the time we'd circled the green a few times I'd told
Meg all about my closest friends, Laura and Ruby, my
crazy family and how I was dreading having to spend the
summer holidays being an unpaid babysitter to my siblings. I kind of realised after a while that I'd been doing
most of the talking, though. It wasn't that Meg was quiet,
more that she kept asking questions about me, and she
didn't volunteer very much information about herself.
She didn't mention her dad, and she didn't seem to want
to talk about why she and her mum had moved to Carrickbeg.

'Hannah!' It was Mum calling. 'I need you!'

'I'll only be a minute,' I told Meg. I was surprised Mum
had actually remembered that she'd promised to call me in
in case I needed to escape.

'It's OK, Mum,' I told her as I reached the door. 'Meg's
really nice, I don't need you to call me in.'

'What? Oh, that's good,' Mum said, 'but actually, I need
you anyway, I'm afraid. I've just remembered the boys are
supposed to be going to a birthday party, and I've just put
Emma down for a nap. Can you mind her and Maisie
while I bring the boys?'

'OK.' I looked back at Meg, who suddenly looked kind

of lonely. 'Is it OK if I ask Meg to come in?'

'Yes, of course. Hurry up though, I really need to get going. We should have been there ten minutes ago.'

I called to Meg and started taking off my rollerblades as I explained to her that big sister duty was calling again.

'Mum says you can come in and hang out with me while I'm babysitting,' I told her quickly.

'Really? That would be great!' Her face fell. 'Oh, I'd better not actually, Sadie is coming over soon.'

'Oh, yeah.' I felt disappointed. 'How about we meet up later, then? We can call for Ruby too.'

'Great! Let's do that.'

I watched as Meg skated back to her own house. Then Maisie called me to come and play teddies.

Not teddies again! I thought to myself, trying to suppress a sigh.

The morning had turned out better than I had been expecting, and I felt pretty sure I had made a new friend in Meg. Maybe she could help me with my summer project – whatever it turned out to be. One thing was for sure, I needed to come up with something fast, or this babysitting thing could turn into a full-time job.

Chapter Three

All the time I was minding the girls, my mind was busily working away on a plan. Mum called me right after she dropped the boys at the party and said since she was out anyway she might as well go to Tesco, and did I mind looking after the girls for a bit longer? I said I didn't mind and she could go ahead. It was true, I didn't mind, not really. Being the oldest in the family does mean you have to help out sometimes, and I do actually like playing with Maisie and looking after Emma. I just didn't want the whole holidays to go by without me having done anything except play teddies, find lost soothers and break up rows. That would make a pretty boring 'What I did in my holidays' essay when I went back to school.

I kept thinking of Meg, all alone next door. It must be strange to move somewhere new and leave all your friends behind. I've lived in Carrickbeg all my life and I can't really imagine what it would be like if Mum and Dad suddenly announced we were moving to a new town. I'd miss Ruby and Laura so much and all the things we do together. I wondered if Meg was missing her friends and her old life.

I saw a stylish-looking older lady with short, neat grey hair making her way up Meg's driveway. She was wearing high heels and a brightly coloured pashmina fastened at the front with a diamanté brooch. I could see why Meg called her Sadie – it was hard to imagine anyone calling her Granny.

Unbelievably, Maisie was tired of teddies. 'Will you read to me?' she asked.

'OK,' I agreed. 'Go and get your Secret Seven book.' We were working our way through the Secret Seven series together. I'd really enjoyed those books when I was a bit younger, and now it was nice to get a chance to read them again and see Maisie enjoying them too.

It was when we were curled up together reading about the adventures of Peter, Janet and all the rest that my super, brilliant, fantastic idea came to me. We should form a club! We'd need a clubhouse of some kind, and a secret password, and ways to get messages to each other. We'd each have our own job to do, and we'd hold regular meetings, and keep records in a secret journal.

'Han – nah!' Maisie was using her whiniest voice. I realised I'd stopped reading.

'Sorry, Maisie! I was just daydreaming there for a minute,' I told her. 'Why don't you read a little bit now, and I'll listen? I'll help you if you get stuck.'

Maisie took the book and started reading. My mind wandered off again. What would we do in the club, though? I was old enough to realise that the type of mysteries that the Secret Seven and the Five Findouters were always solving didn't really crop up like that all the time in real life. I wasn't sure I was cut out for life as a detective, anyway. Sitting in a café spying on people might be fun, but I wasn't so keen on the idea of snooping round old cottages in the dead of night, or trying to stay hidden while following someone on a bike, or having to dress up as a tramp to listen in on secret conversations.

Then I thought about wanting to go to drama camp. Was there some way I could put the ideas together? We wouldn't have a teacher, of course, or even a big group, but was there something we could do on our own?

'HANNAH!' Maisie was stuck on a word and I hadn't noticed.

'OK, Maisie, show me where you've got to,' I told her. I'd just have to work out the details later. But I felt the surge of happiness that having a new plan always brings.

As soon as Mum got home I hopped over the garden wall to knock on Meg's front door. The older lady I'd seen going in earlier answered it.

'Hello, I'm Hannah, I live next door. I just wanted a quick word with Meg if that's all right.'

The lady smiled. 'I'm Sadie. Nice to meet you, Hannah.' She called over her shoulder to Meg, who appeared from the kitchen. 'Don't be too long, Meg. I'm just putting lunch on the table.'

'Sorry to interrupt,' I said to Meg. 'I was just wondering if you can come over this afternoon?'

'Sure,' she said. 'What have you got in mind?'

'I'll explain everything later. Come over to my house about 2.30, OK?'

'See you then!' Meg said, smiling as she closed the door.

Now I just needed to get hold of the other two. I looked at my watch. Still only one o'clock, so I couldn't call over for Ruby just yet. I could drop a note in for her though, so she'd see it as soon as she got home from ballet camp. I'd have to call Laura from the landline at home. Ruby and I reckon we are the only twelve-year-olds in the entire country who don't have mobile phones. Mum says I don't need one until I go to secondary school next year. Laura has one, but she says it's not much use when she can't text her two best friends.

I just had time to phone Laura and tell her about the plan, then I rushed to help Mum unpack the groceries and make the lunch. The boys were getting a lift home from the party, so at least she didn't have to worry about that.

Mum said it was fine if I asked the girls over that after-noon, and she promised to keep Maisie occupied if I wanted to use my room. I wasn't so sure about that one. Keeping Maisie occupied is not easy, especially when you have three other children to look after too. I decided the garden was the best option, unless it started raining or something.

At quarter past two, I dragged the garden table into the middle of the lawn. Actually, that's where it's supposed to live, but the boys keep moving it because it gets in the way of their games. I set up four chairs and got a cloth to wipe away all the cobwebs – it had been a while since we used it, and it looked like the spiders had taken it over. I got out my notebook and pen, and I filled a jug with juice and put it on a tray with four glasses.

The doorbell rang and I rushed to answer it.

'Hey,' said Ruby. 'I got your note – hope you don't mind me being early!'

'No, it's great! Come on in – you can help me with the biscuits and stuff.'

Ruby followed me in, saying hello to Mum and Emma as she passed. I've known Ruby since we were three years old. Our mothers met at toddler group. I'm maybe not as close to her as I am to Laura, but that's not because we don't get on or anything. It's really just because Ruby spends so much of her time on her ballet. As well as the normal classes she gets extra one-on-one lessons from the head of the ballet school, and she seems to spend most of the school holidays at a ballet camp. When she has a show coming up she has all these extra rehearsals, and she's forever doing exercises or stretches or something at home too. Ballet is the number one thing in her life, and Laura and I and her other friends are always going to come second to that. We don't mind though. We're really proud of Ruby, and when she is free to hang out with us, she's great fun.

Laura is super-talented too. Like I explained to Meg, she wants to be a writer when she grows up. Actually, she's a writer already, just not a published one yet. She goes through these dreamy phases when she's starting a new story, and gets completely caught up in the world of her characters. The rest of the time though, she's pretty normal, and she doesn't let it take over her life in quite the same way as Ruby's ballet does.

I don't have a special talent like my two best friends. Sometimes I wonder, if I got the right training and practised really really hard, if I could be good at drama. When I read a book or see a film that I love, I sometimes imagine myself playing that part, and what it would be like to be on the stage.

Ruby had just finished emptying a packet of biscuits onto a plate when the doorbell rang again. I was glad to see it was Laura – I wanted to tell them both about Meg before she got here.

'Hey, come on in! We're just waiting for Meg, then

we've got the full group,' I told her.

'Oh, who's Meg?' Laura asked.

'She just moved in next door. I only met her this morning, but she's really nice.' I watched Laura's face carefully.
When we were younger, she used to be a bit jealous if she
thought I was making new friends without her. She'd kind
of grown out of that, but I still felt a bit nervous. I didn't
want her deciding she didn't like Meg before she'd even
met her.

I needn't have worried, though. 'Oh, that's great,' Laura
said. 'Remember you were worried it would be more
screaming brats moving in next door!'

In the kitchen, Bobby was showing Ruby his latest
kick-boxing move.

'Look, Ruby, you stand here,' he instructed her. 'Now
watch.'

He took a couple of steps back, then screeched, 'Hi –
YA!' and came running towards her, jumping and kicking
his leg in the air at the same time.

Ruby screamed and then giggled. 'Wow, Bobby. You're
getting really good at that.'

'Why don't you show Zach?' I suggested.

'But I want to show Ruby what comes next,' Bobby
said.

'Another time maybe. I need Ruby now,' I told him.

'OK,' Bobby sighed. He went running off, shouting to

Zach to come and practise with him.

'Quick, let's go outside before they come back,' I said.

I picked up the tray and Ruby opened the patio door so I could carry it out to the back garden. I liked being the host – it made me feel very grown-up.

We settled down at the table.

'So what's this big plan you mentioned?' Ruby wanted to know. 'It sounded really mysterious in your note.'

'Yeah, I'm dying to know too. Your plans are always either completely brilliant, or else they land us in a lot of trouble,' Laura said with a laugh.

'Like the time you decided we should have a yard sale to surprise our parents, only you sold a whole lot of things you weren't supposed to,' Ruby giggled.

'Like your dad's favourite tie,' Laura said. 'And your mum's sunglasses.'

'And a cake tin belonging to your granny,' Ruby said.

'And the book my mum was in the middle of reading,' Laura added.

'The book was your idea!' I pointed out. I pretended to be cross. 'Fine, if you don't want to hear my brilliant plan, I won't tell you.'

'Of course we do,' Laura said in a soothing tone. 'We'll just be a bit better prepared this time, and put all our valuables in a safe place.'

'Please tell us, I'm dying to hear now!' Ruby said.

'I'll tell you everything when Meg gets here,' I promised. 'Actually, it's only the start of a plan. I need you guys to help me turn it into a proper one.'

'Hey.' It was Meg, peeping over the hedge between our two gardens, and looking a little shy.

'Hi, Meg! Have you found the secret passage in our garden?'

It wasn't really a secret passage, but I was still in an Enid Blyton kind of mood. I showed her the gap in the hedge where she could squeeze through. It's my favourite sneaky hiding place when I'm playing hide and seek with my brothers.

'This is great!' Meg said, emerging from the hedge into our garden. 'So much handier than going all the way round to the front door.'

I brought her over to the table where the others were looking at her curiously, Laura shading her eyes from the sun with her hand.

'This is Ruby, and this is Laura,' I said. 'Guys, this is Meg.'

'Hi,' they all said.

'Meg just moved in next door,' I explained.

'Are your parents busy unpacking?' Ruby said.

'Oh, it's just me and Mum,' Meg said.

'My parents are separated too,' Laura told her. 'It sucks at first, but you kind of get used to it.'

A funny look crossed Meg's face. I had already worked

out that she wasn't ready to talk about whatever was going on in her family, so I thought I'd better change the subject.

'So I wanted you all to come over because I've got this idea,' I said. 'I think we should form a club.'

I sat back, waiting for them all to exclaim in delight at the idea.

No one said anything.

'What kind of a club?' Laura asked at last.

'This isn't going to be one of your Secret Seven type ideas again, is it?' Ruby said, sounding sceptical.

I remembered then that I'd tried to set up a club with Ruby and Laura ages ago. It was supposed to be like the Secret Seven, but as there were only three of us I christened us the Terrific Three. We made membership badges and drew up a club code, and we had to use a secret password to get into each other's bedrooms. The idea kind of fizzled out when we realised there just weren't any mysteries out there which we could solve. Well, not unless you count the mystery of who had stolen Laura's Easter egg, and we already knew that the answer to that was her big sister Andrea, except we couldn't prove it because she'd eaten the evidence.

'Of course not,' I said, trying to sound as dignified as possible. 'We were only little kids then. This is something different. We'd have regular meetings, and we'd all have different jobs in the club. It would be kind of like a summer project, only a fun one, not like you have in school, and our parents would have to let us meet up with each other because it would be club business.'

'I like that idea,' Ruby said slowly. 'I mean, ballet camp is going to take up a lot of my time, so if I want to see you guys it would be good to have something I need to go to so Mum doesn't say "oh, not now", or "maybe after dinner" or whatever.'

'Yes, but ...' said Laura, '... you still haven't said what we're actually going to DO.'

'Well, here's the thing,' I said. I was almost afraid to say the next part in case they didn't like it. 'You know the way I was really hoping to go to drama camp ... well, I just thought, why don't we have a sort of drama camp of our own? Ruby, you know all about being on the stage because of your ballet, and Laura, you're really good at writing, so you could help us come up with scripts and things like that. And Meg likes acting too, so we've got everything we need.'

I stopped talking and looked around to see everyone's reaction.

'I think it's a great idea!' Meg said. 'We could have rehearsals and plan a show. Laura could write something for us, or we could just adapt a story we know, like a fairytale or something.'

I smiled at her in relief and looked at the other two.

They were smiling too – phew!

'Brilliant,' Laura said.

'I love it,' Ruby said.

I couldn't help bouncing up and down in my chair. 'Yay! I can't wait to get started!'

Chapter Four

'Right,' I said. 'We need to decide a few things. Like, what's our name going to be? Where are we going to meet? How often should we meet? What's the first thing we should focus on?'

Mum says I can be a bit bossy sometimes. I do try not to be. But I'm good at organising things and getting things done. And, without wanting to sound conceited or anything, I do have a lot of good ideas.

'Well, we can meet in each other's gardens as long as the weather's OK,' Ruby said. 'Maybe we can take it in turns to be the host.'

'I wish we had a clubhouse,' I said. 'I don't suppose anyone has an old garden shed they've forgotten to tell me about?'

'No, and if we did it would be full of junk,' Laura said.

'Anyway, outdoors is going to be better than a shed. We'll need a lot of space for acting,' Meg said. She sounded like she knew what she was talking about.

'OK, that makes sense,' I admitted. 'So how often should

we meet?'

'Obviously, the answer is as often as possible. Is twice a day too much?' Laura asked innocently.

The others laughed. 'I think that might be a bit much even for Hannah,' Ruby said. 'How about three times a week to get started and we'll see how that goes?'

'That sounds good,' I said. 'But can we meet again tomorrow just so we can get started properly? That'll give us all a bit of time to come up with some more ideas. Like what we're going to do. I don't want us to just sit around talking about acting, I want us to actually do something!'

'We could put on a show for our parents and grannies and grandads,' suggested Laura.

'Or something for the little kids on the green that would keep them entertained,' said Ruby.

'We could charge a small entrance fee and give the money to charity,' said Meg.

Soon everyone was talking at once, wanting to share all their ideas for our new club. By the time Ruby's little brother called around to say their mum wanted her home, we had a definite agenda for our next meeting. We'd elect club officers (that was my idea), decide on a club name (my idea too), and plan a schedule of meetings and where they would be held (also my idea. Actually, I may as well admit that most of the ideas were mine). Meg said that everyone should bring along some suggestions about what we'd like to act in, and we could talk about that too.

This was so exciting. I couldn't wait to really get started.

After the others had all left I got out a new notebook and my favourite sparkly pen. I had a whole stack of unused notebooks on my bookshelf, because people are always giving me them as presents – probably because they know I like organising things and making plans. I chose one with a pink cover decorated with silver stars. It looked like the perfect kind of notebook for starting a drama club.

Soon my hand hurt from writing, I had scribbled down so much. I had so many ideas my hand could hardly keep up! I just hoped I'd be able to read them the next day. My handwriting isn't the neatest anyway, and when I'm in a huge hurry to get everything down it can get pretty scribbly.

After a while I realised I'd better go down and help Mum – it was getting to that time of day when she's trying to make the dinner, Emma is cranky because she's hungry, Maisie keeps getting under her feet, and the boys start fighting. So I took them all out to the garden and organised a big game of hide and seek to keep them occupied. Even Emma joined in, though I had to carry her on my hip, and she wasn't much good at staying quiet, so we ended up doing most of the seeking.

'Thanks, Hannah,' Mum said, kissing me on the top of the head as we trooped in for dinner. 'I don't know what I'd do without you.'

I felt a bit guilty. Would it make things harder for Mum if I started spending as much time as I wanted to on the club?

It seemed like three o'clock the next day would NEVER arrive. I decided to pop over to Meg's after breakfast so I could tell her some of my ideas, but when I rang the doorbell her mum, Cordelia, told me they were about to go shopping. Cordelia was young and very glamorous-looking, with blonde hair like Meg's and designer sun-glasses perched on top of her head. She was the sort of person who called everyone darling (even me, who she'd only just met) and she spoke so quickly it almost made my head spin.

'So sorry for stealing her away, Hannah darling!' she said with a smile. 'But it's quite the clothing emergency! Meg simply has nothing to wear!'

'Don't exaggerate, Mum,' Meg said. 'I just need some warm stuff,' she told me. 'Pretty much all I packed was light dresses, shorts and T-shirts. So we've got to stock up on leggings and hoodies and stuff.'

'And I simply must find something more suitable to

wear for my interviews,' Cordelia added. 'I mean, tell me truly, Hannah darling, would you offer me a job in this sort of outfit?'

I thought she looked pretty amazing in her lightweight white jumper, skinny jeans and high-heeled boots, but I didn't need to say anything as Cordelia immediately answered her own question. 'Of course you wouldn't! It's absolutely essential that one looks the part when applying for a job in an office. I'm a little out of practice, but I'm sure with the right look I'll be able to convince someone to take me on.'

'Hannah, have you seen Maisie?' It was Mum, standing at our garden wall and shading her eyes from the sun.

'No – has she disappeared again?' Maisie has a habit of disappearing when someone is annoying her, and she seems to go completely deaf to anyone calling her. 'I'll come and help you look for her.'

'Sorry to interrupt,' Mum said to Cordelia. 'I'm Claire, by the way.'

'Cordelia,' Meg's mum told her, extending a long elegant arm to shake hands across the garden wall. 'So nice to meet you.'

'You must come over for coffee some day,' Mum said, smoothing down her hair a little self-consciously. 'I'd ask you in now, but I'm afraid the place is a bit of a mess.'

'Oh, don't worry, darling, we're off to the shops just

now anyway. Meg here has got absolutely nothing to wear – I'd forgotten how changeable the Irish summers can be.'

'I'm sure summers were much nicer when we were young,' Mum agreed.

Meg and I grinned at each other – that was exactly the kind of thing parents always say.

'Mustn't keep you,' Cordelia said to Mum. 'Come along, Meg, darling.'

'There's something familiar about her,' Mum said, watching them drive away. 'Where did you say they used to live?'

'I'm not actually sure. But Cordelia grew up in Carrickbeg – maybe you knew her when you were kids?'

'Maybe.' Mum had already moved on. 'I'd better go and look for Maisie. I can't think where she's got to.'

'I'll help you,' I said.

I headed upstairs, still wondering about Meg and her family. I couldn't help being curious, but I didn't want to pry. Someone like Tracey Dunne would have just come right out and asked Meg where they used to live, and why they'd moved, and where her dad was, and she wouldn't have stopped until Meg told her everything she needed to know. Then she'd have used the information against her in one of her nasty little schemes. I knew Meg didn't need that kind of pressure. Whatever was going on, Meg would tell us when she was ready. Sometimes talking is what being friends is all about, but sometimes being a good friend means knowing when to shut up too.

I found Maisie in the first place I looked – our room, where she was sitting on her bed, arms folded and bottom lip stuck out.

'Mum, she's here,' I shouted down the stairs. 'Maisie, didn't you hear Mum calling?'

Maisie unfolded her arms so that she could pointedly fold them again to let me know she was cross. I tried not to smile.

'What's the matter?'

'Zach and Bobby are playing *Star Wars* again and they said I can only play if I'm Princess Leia. I want to be Luke Skywalker, but Bobby says he's *always* Luke Skywalker. Then I said I'd be Rey instead, but Zach said they're not playing that bit today. It's not fair, they're always ganging up on me!'

I'd been involved in enough *Star Wars* arguments to know there was no point in trying to interfere. 'Why don't you and I play something else?' I suggested instead. 'A board game?'

'OK – can we play Monopoly?'

Maisie always wants to play Monopoly even though she's only five and she doesn't understand it properly. She keeps putting houses on train stations and charging people extra, and she gets annoyed if anyone else tries to buy the pink section because it's her favourite colour so she thinks she should be the only one allowed to own it.

'Only if you play properly,' I warned her.

'Of course I will.' Maisie was already leading the way downstairs. 'I always play properly. It's other people who don't understand the rules.'

Monopoly is a LONG game. Especially when played the Maisie way. I started to get a bit worried when it got near to lunchtime that it wasn't going to finish, but then I landed on one of Maisie's illegal hotels and she cleared me out of all my cash.

After lunch I ran upstairs to get changed. I felt like the first meeting of a drama club required a dramatic outfit. I tried on lots of different combinations while Maisie watched and gave me her opinion. Soon most of my clothes were in a pile on my bed. Finally we settled on denim shorts over purple tights, a black top with seagulls printed all over it and a deep pink cardigan.

'You need something with feathers too.' Maisie was very definite on that point. 'Feathers are dramatic.'

She rummaged around in her bedside locker and pulled out a hairslide with big pink feathers on it. She insisted on me trying it on. Actually, it looked pretty good.

'Now do I look dramatic enough?' I asked her.

'You look great!' she said with a big smile.

'Thanks, Maisie.' I gave her a hug.

Maisie's smile had turned a bit wistful. 'Can I come to your meeting too, or is it just for big girls?'

'Sorry, Maisie. It's just for big girls,' I told her. I felt bad – she was so interested in the whole idea. 'I'll tell you all about it when I get home, OK? And if we're doing a show maybe you can help me with my costume.'

'OK,' Maisie said, sighing.

I looked at my watch. 'I'd better get going!' We were meeting at Ruby's house today, and I'd said I'd call for Meg first. I grabbed my notebook and pen and raced down the stairs.

Chapter Five

Cordelia answered the door. She was wearing a navy pin-stripe jacket and matching knee-length skirt and a white blouse, and she looked so different from earlier that I couldn't help staring.

'Hannah, what do you think?' she said, giving a little twirl.

'Lovely,' I said.

'Now you would definitely want to hire me, wouldn't you?' Cordelia beamed. 'Heavens, imagine me holding down a nine-to-five job! It's too funny!'

'You haven't got the job yet, Mum,' Meg said as she appeared behind her. 'You still need to do the interview.'

'Oh, that's just a small detail,' Cordelia said, waving her hand as if the interview was barely worth thinking about now that she had her perfect work outfit. 'What are you girls up to, anyway?'

'We're forming a drama club,' I told her, surprised that Meg hadn't said anything.

Too late I saw the look on Meg's face. For some reason

I didn't understand, she clearly hadn't planned on telling her mum what we were up to.

Cordelia's carefree expression vanished. She looked at Meg, worry etched on her face. 'Oh, Meg, do you think that's a good idea, darling?'

'Really, Mum, it's fine,' Meg told her. 'It's just four girls getting together to share our ideas and stuff. We're not going to be appearing in the town hall or anything like that!'

'My mum says it should keep us out of trouble for a bit,' I joked, trying to lighten the mood. Whatever was going on there was a real tension in the air. Cordelia was still frowning, and Meg wouldn't look at her. She grabbed her hoodie from the bottom of the stairs and stepped out past her.

'Just ... be careful, OK?' Cordelia said.

'I will,' Meg said, sighing.

We walked towards Ruby's. Neither of us said anything for a minute. All the questions were whirling around in my head once again. Why on earth would Meg's mum not want her to be in a drama club? She didn't mind us hanging out together – she certainly didn't seem like one of those mums who thought you should spend all your holidays visiting relatives or something – so what was the problem with the club? Suddenly I found myself blurting out, 'Why didn't you want your mum to know what we're doing?'

'It's ... it's complicated, Hannah,' Meg said, not looking at me. 'I can't really explain it just yet. I will some day, OK?'

'OK,' I said. I didn't know what else I could say. I wished Meg would just tell me what was going on.

Laura was just arriving on her bike when we got to Ruby's. Laura lives a few streets away, and she's allowed to cycle over here to meet up with us. I, on the other hand, am not allowed to cycle over to hers because of crossing the main road. Mum says maybe when I start sixth class in September. I'm not sure how that's going to make it magically safer for me to cross the road, but that's Mum for you. And it's not like Laura is any more careful than me – actually, if anything she's less careful. When she's got a new idea for a story rattling around in her brain she goes into a world of her own and could quite easily cycle right into the road, thinking she was in the middle of a field in wartime France or something like that. But her mum is a bit more laidback than mine about letting her do things. It's probably something to do with her being the youngest instead of the oldest like me.

'Great, you guys are early! Come on in!'

Ruby led the way up to her room, which is the pinkest room in the history of the earth. Everything in it is pink, from the walls to the curtains to the duvet cover, and even the tassles on the lampshade. It's a bit girly for my taste, but it suits Ruby, and it certainly makes the right backdrop to the ballet posters all over her walls.

We all found somewhere to sit. Meg sank into a beanbag on the floor, and Laura sat beside her on a fluffy cushion (pink, of course). I took the desk chair because it made me feel more official, although I turned it around so that I had my back to the desk and was facing the others. Ruby stretched out on her side on her bed, unselfconsciously lifting one leg as high as she could and holding it there, before gracefully lowering it again. She repeated this a few times, hardly seeming aware of what she was doing. I smiled to myself.

'Right,' I said, 'we're all here, so I hereby call to order the first meeting of ... oh. What are we calling ourselves? Maybe that should be the first item on the agenda. Has anyone got any suggestions?'

'How about Woodland Green Drama Club?' Ruby suggested.

'Or Woodland Green Players,' said Meg. 'Drama groups are often called players.'

I tried to think of a tactful way to say I thought it sounded like a pretty boring name, but thankfully Laura came to my rescue.

'That makes it sound like anyone who lives in Woodland Green can join,' she pointed out. 'We don't want that.

Also, you might remember I'm not actually from Woodland Green, so unless you want me to leave and one of
your neighbours to join ...'

'That's a good point, actually,' Meg admitted.

'It's also a bit too ... grown-up,' I said, managing to find a
more diplomatic word than boring. 'We're just kids doing
this for fun, so we should have a fun name.'

'How about something like Fame Club?' suggested
Laura. '*Fame* was this eighties TV show about teenagers
who wanted to be on the stage. My mum used to love it,
she has all the DVDs.'

'It's on the right track, but I think we need an original
idea if we can manage it,' I said.

I was tapping my notebook with my sparkly pen as I
spoke. I glanced down at the starry pattern on the notebook, and that's when inspiration struck. 'How about Star
Club?'

'That's perfect!' Ruby said.

'Yes, I like it,' Laura said slowly. 'It's fun, and it's not too
restrictive. It could include Ruby's ballet as well, not just
drama.'

Meg was nodding too. 'Sounds just right. Nice one,
Hannah.'

I wrote it in big letters at the top of my page: STAR
CLUB. It looked great!

'OK. I hereby call the first meeting of Star Club to

order. Now, has anyone got any ideas for us?'

I was dying to share my ideas, but I was determined not to take over the meeting, so I wanted to let everyone else go first.

'Could we try to put on a ballet?' Ruby said. 'Just a simple one,' she added quickly, seeing all our faces.

'No way,' Laura said. 'I did ballet for two years, and I hated it. I begged Mum to let me stop, and it was only when the teacher told her I had two left feet that she finally gave in. I'm just no good at it.'

'I did a bit of ballet and I was OK at it, but I'm definitely not good enough to be in a show,' Meg said.

'Me neither. Sorry, Ruby,' I said. 'But maybe we can do some sort of variety show, with different acts, and your act could be a ballet dance. Or we could work it into a play some way.'

'Anyway, I thought you'd be glad to do something different,' Laura said. 'It's ballet, ballet, ballet, all day long with you. There are other things in the world, you know. It might do you good to try something else!'

Ruby looked set to argue. She doesn't take criticism of her beloved ballet very well, so I thought I'd better smooth things over.

'We'll all be trying something new here, that's part of the fun,' I said quickly. 'But like I said, I'm sure ballet can come in somewhere. So, any other ideas?'

'How about acting out some scenes from *Little Women*?' Laura said.

'Yes, I thought of *Little Women* too,' I said. 'It would be perfect for us because it's got four sisters in it. And we even have a Meg already – and an aspiring writer.'

'Four girls sounds great. I've been wondering about that, actually,' said Meg. 'Do you think it's going to be a problem that we are all girls? What will we do about parts that should be played by boys?'

Ruby made a face. 'Well, we're not inviting any boys to join, that's for sure!'

Ruby thinks boys are smelly, annoying and generally a huge pain. This comes from having brothers. Mum always smiles and says give her a bit of time and her opinions will soon change. Ruby insists that they won't.

'Let's just keep it to the four of us for now,' I said. 'Maybe in the future we'll need boys to get involved in shows or whatever, but they don't have to be a part of the club. We're just getting started anyway, we need to find out what we really want to do first.'

'There are tons of things we can do that don't need boys, anyway,' Laura said.

'If we do have boys in the story we can play those parts ourselves. That's part of being a good actor,' Meg put in.

'That's OK then,' Ruby said, sounding relieved. 'I've got more than enough boy trouble in my life just now.'

We all laughed.

'So, we'll stick to things that have mostly girl roles for now,' I said. 'Should we do like Laura suggested and use a book for inspiration, or try to write something ourselves?'

'Any talented writers in the house?' Ruby asked, using a pencil case as a pretend loudhailer.

We all looked at Laura, who immediately started blushing. 'I'm working on something, but it's not ready,' she muttered.

'I think it would be good to adapt something from a book so we don't have to start from scratch,' Ruby said. 'I haven't read *Little Women*, but I know you two love it. Or we could do something from Jacqueline Wilson. She has some great girl characters.'

'Or how about Harry Potter?' Laura said.

'Oh that would be brilliant,' I said. 'Although I don't know how we'd manage the magic bits – it might be too tricky.'

We talked a bit about how we'd actually go about adapting scenes from a book. It seemed like a lot of work for one person.

'Why don't we pick a story we like, and when we know what characters we're playing we can all write their lines?' Meg said.

'I like that idea. A joint effort,' Ruby said.

'It can be sort of improvised, as well,' Meg said. Seeing

puzzled looks, she explained, 'That means you make it up as you go along.'

'Oh, oh, oh!' Ruby suddenly sat bolt upright on her bed, her stretches forgotten. 'I know! We can do *Ballet Shoes*! You know the one by Noel Streatfeild? There are three sisters in that, and the fourth person could be the teacher or the nanny, maybe. It's perfect.'

'Plus, you know, there's ballet in it,' Laura said with a grin.

'Well, that too,' Ruby admitted. 'I just love the scene where Posy goes to audition for Manoff. I feel like I know exactly how she feels.'

Ruby's eyes were shining, and I had to admit she'd come up with a fantastic idea.

'Is it all about ballet?' Meg wanted to know.

She sounded a bit sceptical, so I rushed to reassure her.

'No, it's about three sisters who are orphans and they go to a theatre school. Pauline is the oldest – she loves acting. The youngest one, Posy, loves ballet, and the middle one, Petrova, isn't really interested in any of it, but she has to learn it anyway, because they need to earn a living.'

'Definitely not just ballet,' Laura chimed in. I was glad to see her sticking up for Ruby's idea. 'There's all the stuff with the tenants in their house, and about the way the sisters get on together and with their guardian and everything.'

'You'd love it,' I promised. 'There's loads about the theatre in it, and about how Pauline really wants to be an actress. I'll lend you my copy so you can see for yourself.'

'OK, well, it sounds great,' Meg said. 'Let's go for it!'

'YAY!' shouted Ruby, turning head over heels off the bed and finishing up by doing the splits, her arms held gracefully over her head.

'OK, how about we all pick out our favourite bits for the next time we met up?' I suggested. 'Then we can decide who's going to play who.'

I already knew who I wanted to play and was hoping no one else would have the same idea, but I didn't say anything about it yet.

Laura looked at her watch. 'Have we talked about everything?' she asked. 'I need to get home soon – Mum said I have to help Andrea with dinner.'

Laura's mum works full time, so often the two girls help with stuff around the house. Andrea is the oldest – she's sixteen – so she does more than Laura, but Laura's pretty good for doing her share too.

I looked down at my notebook. 'What about when we should meet, and where? Should we pick a few set days every week?'

'I think we should just meet as often as we can during the holidays,' Meg said.

'Yes, that makes sense,' Laura said. 'We'll probably need

a stricter schedule once we're back at school,' (Ruby groaned) 'but none of us have anything else on at the moment.'

'Apart from me,' Ruby pointed out. 'I've got ballet camp in the mornings, but I'm free in the afternoons, so can we have the meetings then?'

Everyone was fine with this. I suggested that we could take it in turns to host the meeting, though I did wonder how I would get to Laura's house if Mum wouldn't let me take my bike.

'We can meet in my house next time,' Meg said.

'Are you sure your mum won't mind?' I asked, thinking of her reaction earlier.

'Not if I don't tell her,' Meg said. 'She's going to be out doing interviews a lot in the next few days, so she won't be at home.'

I obviously still looked concerned, because Meg said, 'Really, don't worry. I don't know what got into her earlier, she's normally fine about stuff like this. I'll clear everything up before she gets home, anyway, so it'll be fine. What's next?'

'OK – last thing on the agenda. Electing officers,' I said. 'We can probably wait to appoint people to be in charge of wardrobe, and props, and all that sort of thing until we know more about what we're doing, but I think we should have a director, anyway, to sort of make sure things are moving in the right direction.'

'Hmmm, that's a tricky one,' Laura said, putting her chin in her hands and pretending to think deeply. 'Who has the right skills to be in charge of our club?'

'It's not being in charge,' I said quickly. 'This is a democracy, we'll vote on everything. It's just a sort of ... leader, I suppose.'

'Let's think about that one,' Laura said, frowning thoughtfully.

I shifted uncomfortably in my chair. I'd done my best not to be too bossy, but maybe I'd put people off already. I was always doing that without meaning to. And Meg certainly seemed to know a lot more about theatre than I did. Maybe they'd rather have her in as director of the club.

'The perfect leader ...' Laura said, her face breaking into a smile as she looked from Meg to Ruby and then back to me.

'Hannah,' all three of them said at once.

I couldn't help smiling too. 'If you're sure ...' I said.

'Yes!' Laura told me. 'You can get yourself one of those director's boards that say "Take 57" on it if you like! Now I'd really better get going. See you at Meg's tomorrow!'

Chapter Six

I was kind of sorry I'd offered to lend Meg my copy of *Ballet Shoes*, because I realised I'd need a copy to look over myself. Anyway, I'd already promised, so I went to drop it in to her right after dinner.

I thought it might be better not to disturb her mum in case she was still trying to avoid telling her about Star Club, so I squeezed through the hedge and sneaked around the back of the house, hoping to see Meg through a window. Luckily she was in the family room on her own. I tapped gently on the window and Meg looked up and smiled, coming over straight away to kneel up on the window seat and open the window.

'I brought the book,' I said. 'I thought I'd come through the garden instead of disturbing your mum.'

'That hole in the hedge is going to come in really handy,' Meg giggled.

'So is she OK about the club?' I asked.

Meg shrugged. 'I don't really know. She had a couple of phone calls after I got home so I haven't really been talking to her. I'm kind of hoping she'll be too busy to think about it.'

Suddenly I heard her mum calling her name. Instinctively I ducked below the window. I heard the door open and Cordelia saying, 'Time for dinner, honey.'

'OK, Mum, just coming,' Meg said. She waited for her mum to leave, then leaned out the window. 'I'd better go.'

'Me too,' I said. 'See you tomorrow!'

I was glad I didn't have to go past the kitchen window to get to our garden. Walking home, I remembered that I'd seen at least one copy of *Ballet Shoes* in the library. The library is one of the places I never have to argue with Mum to be allowed go to. For one thing, she likes to encourage reading as much as she can (not that she has to try hard with me). For another, it's only about a five minute walk away, with no main roads to cross.

I decided I'd head up to the library first thing in the morning. I could even offer to bring some of my brothers and sisters with me so Mum could go to Tiny Tunes, the baby music class, with Emma. I knew it was one of the things she missed during the summer holidays – not because of singing 'Row, Row, Row Your Boat' five hundred times in a row, but because afterwards the adults got to have a cup of tea and a chat while the babies crawled around and played with the tambourines and xylophones and bells.

Mum liked meeting up with the other parents, but she couldn't very well drag Maisie, Bobby and Zach along, so she usually just gave it a miss when we weren't in school. This time though, I'd tell her she should go. And there was something in it for me as well – if I'd minded the others all morning, surely she wouldn't mind if I spent the afternoon at the club meeting at Meg's.

Mum was all in favour of the plan, so the next morning she and Emma headed off to Tiny Tunes. I rounded up Maisie, Bobby and Zach for our library trip. Actually, that makes it sound a lot easier than it was.

First of all Maisie couldn't find her shoes, and instead of looking properly for them she trailed around the house, as if expecting them to pop out from somewhere. Next Bobby couldn't find the library books he wanted to return.

'Where did you have them last?' I asked patiently.

'I don't know,' Bobby said. 'I think Zach borrowed them.'

'No I didn't!' Zach said. 'I wouldn't read your babyish old books anyway.'

It was about to turn into a full-blown row, so I sent them into separate rooms to search there, while I started a search of my own. I found Maisie's shoes (in the laundry basket) and Bobby's library books (one underneath a cushion on the couch, and the other, surprise surprise, right in plain view on Zach's locker).

At long last we were ready. The walk to the library took us approximately one-tenth of the time it took us to actually leave the house. I quickly got Maisie settled down with some crayons and colouring pages and sent Zach off to explore the science section and Bobby to pick out a new novel. I sat down with *Ballet Shoes* and started reading.

I soon found myself totally lost in the story. I loved all three of the Fossil girls, and as I was reading I was picturing how they should be played on stage. Petrova is so independent-minded and way more interested in cars than in anything to do with the theatre. Posy has this amazing self-confidence and her only focus in life is her ballet. Pauline has all the sense of responsibility of being the oldest and she is also the one who is head over heels in love with the theatre and wants to learn all she can about being on the stage.

They were all such great characters, but there was no doubt in my mind which one I wanted to play. From the very first time I read *Ballet Shoes* (and this, I reckoned, would be my seventh time to read it) I had identified with Pauline.

Our lives were worlds apart. There was Pauline living in London, nearly a century ago and attending a professional theatre school. And here was I in this small Irish suburb, not even able to go to drama camp and just planning a little show with my friends. But our dreams were the same – filled with bright lights and sweeping curtains and the thrill of stepping on to a stage.

I really hoped no one else would want to be Pauline. Ruby would be Posy, of course, that was obvious. Either Meg or Laura would be great as Petrova – but what if one of them would prefer to be Pauline? As I imagined what it would be like to have to watch someone else playing the part I wanted so much I almost felt like crying. We were a team, of course we were, and we'd have to agree on it together – I knew I couldn't go making demands or this club was never going to work out. I just had to hope no one else would want the part as much as I did.

I was so totally absorbed in my thoughts that I'd pretty much forgotten where I was until a shadow fell across my book.

'Some babysitter you are!'

Standing over me was my arch-enemy – the horrible Tracey Dunne. 'You shouldn't bring those little brats out if you can't control them!'

'What do you mean?' I scrambled to my feet, the book abandoned on the seat beside me. 'What's going on?'

'Your stupid little brother thinks he owns the library. I think you need to explain to him that these books belong to everyone!' Tracy stood with her hands on her hips and glared at me.

I hurried over to the aisle where I'd left Zach looking through some encyclopaedias. He was holding grimly on to a book while Tracey's little brother Tyler (who is nearly as horrible as she is) tried to grab it. Zach's face was red and his jaw was clenched in determination, and I could tell he was on the verge of tears. Even though he's older Zach is way more sensitive than Bobby, who would probably just have told Tyler to get lost.

'Hannah!' His voice wobbled. 'I had this first. Really I did. And Tyler just tried to take it off me.'

'He's had it for ages!' Tyler whined. 'It's not his! I need it!'

He gave an extra hard tug on the book. To my horror there was a loud sound of paper tearing and the book ripped right in half.

Zach immediately burst into tears. I put my arm around him and tried to comfort him, all the while looking at the damaged book and wondering what on earth we were going to do.

I heard the swift patter of feet from behind the bookshelves and one of the library staff appeared. My heart sank. Just our luck that it wasn't the nice young red-haired lady who often helps me choose books. No, it had to be Mr Jenkins, the grumpiest and meanest librarian who ever lived.

'What's going on here?' he asked.

'Look what you've done, Zach!' Tracey said. 'This is all your fault! If you had shared nicely with Tyler this would never have happened.'

Zach was crying too hard to answer.

'It's not his fault,' I told Mr Jenkins, trying my best to speak calmly. 'Zach was reading this book first, and Tyler tried to take it from him.'

'I was just asking him to share it!' Tyler said. 'I want to learn all about dinosaurs too! I just asked him to share it and he pulled it away so hard it tore!'

'Yes, that's exactly what happened, I was watching,' Tracey said.

'That's not true!' I exclaimed, shocked at the bare-faced lie. 'Tyler was the one who tried to pull it away from Zach!'

'Sounds to me like you're both to blame,' Mr Jenkins snapped. 'Well, the book will have to be paid for. Where are your parents?'

'My mum's not here,' I said. 'I'm looking after Zach.'

'And I'm looking after Tyler, but I was actually keeping an eye on him, not like Hannah who was all the way over there, ignoring her brother,' Tracey said. 'That's how I know what really happened.'

'Well, you'll both have to come up to the desk and show me your library cards so I can put it on your accounts,' Mr Jenkins said. 'There'll be no more borrowing books until that fine is paid.'

I trailed after him, my arm still around Zach. I was furious that Zach was being blamed in the wrong, but there didn't seem to be anything we could do – it was Tracey's word against mine.

We stood at the desk while Mr Jenkins made a great show of bringing up the right files on the computer, grumbling all the while about young people today having no respect for library property. I felt a little tug on my sleeve. Bobby was standing there with a big pile of books in his arms.

'Not now, Bobby,' I whispered.

I didn't know whether Mr Jenkins was going to ban us all from taking out books, or just Zach.

'Hannah ...' Bobby said, tugging at my sleeve urgently.

'I said not now!' I repeated in a fierce whisper.

I wondered how much the book would cost to replace. It was a big encyclopaedia so it was probably pretty expensive. Even if Tyler was going to have to pay half of it, I wasn't sure I had enough money for Zach's share.

Mr Jenkins was still muttering away. 'Disgraceful behaviour ... completely careless ... think they'd been brought up in a zoo ... not like in my day ...'

'But Hannah!' Bobby said loudly.

'SHUSH!' said Mr Jenkins. 'No shouting in the library!'

Bobby ignored him. 'Hannah, I can't find Maisie.'

Chapter Seven

With a jump I realised how long it was since I'd seen Maisie. I had been so caught up in the book, and then in the row, that I hadn't even glanced over to the table where she'd been colouring.

Tracey sniggered. 'You really shouldn't be allowed out. Those children need a proper babysitter. You know, one who doesn't let them tear up books, and generally knows where they are?'

I ignored her. 'Stay here,' I ordered Zach and Bobby.

'Hey!' shouted Mr Jenkins, forgetting his own rule about not shouting in the library. 'Where do you think you're going – I haven't finished!'

I ignored him too. I rushed over to the children's section. No Maisie at the colouring table, no Maisie at the comfy chairs along the window. No Maisie in any of the book aisles. No Maisie in front of the audiobooks and DVDs.

I checked the toilets, even though I didn't really think Maisie would have gone in there on her own – she's scared of the noisy handdryers. No one there either.

I was starting to panic now. Where could she have got to? Surely she wouldn't have left the library all on her own – would she? Maisie was a daydreamer – what if she got it into her head that we'd gone home without her, and decided to follow us?

I rushed to the window and looked out onto the road. The first thing that caught my eye was the church hall where Mum had taken Emma to Tiny Tunes. Could Maisie have tried to go there to find Mum? It was on the other side of the road, across four lanes of traffic.

I felt sick with fear. Maisie was only five – there was no way she should be out on her own, never mind trying to cross a busy street. Desperate, I ran back over to the desk.

'Now look here …' Mr Jenkins began once again.

'Don't tell me you've lost another one!' Tracey could hardly keep the glee out of her voice.

'What's going on?'

I could have cried with relief. Rebecca, the nice young red-haired librarian, was standing behind Mr Jenkins, a look of true concern on her face.

'I've lost Maisie,' I told her, trying to hold back the tears. 'I've searched the children's section, and I can't find her anywhere.'

Zach had pretty much stopped crying about the book, but looked like he was on the verge of crying about Maisie instead, and even Bobby wasn't far behind him.

'Don't worry, I'm sure she hasn't gone far,' Rebecca said. Her voice was so calm and kind that I felt reassured at once. 'Now, why don't you two boys come and sit down over here with your books, and I'll help Hannah look for Maisie.'

Taking absolutely no notice of grumpy old Mr Jenkins, Rebecca steered the two boys over to a couch in a central spot where we'd be able to keep an eye on them. She turned back to me. 'Now, she's definitely not in the children's section?'

'No. I looked everywhere,' I told her, my voice trembling.

'And she's not in the toilet?'

'No, I looked there too.'

'Then let's try the adult section. She may have wandered over there looking for you.'

Rebecca led the way, calm and efficient. I was so glad to have someone else take charge. I followed behind her, my eyes darting all over, hoping Maisie would just suddenly appear.

Rebecca walked along one side of the rows of shelves and I walked down the other. I even looked under the shelves, just in case Maisie was hiding under there for some reason. I spotted discarded books, an empty water bottle, and lots and lots of dust – but absolutely no sign of a cute little five-year-old with blonde plaits and a blue dress.

I was just beginning to feel a bit frantic when I heard Rebecca calling. 'Hannah!' I knew from her voice that it was good news. 'Over here!'

I found Rebecca standing in the doorway to a room at the back of the library. It was a big bright room, normally used for book clubs and meetings and talks.

Rebecca turned to me with a big smile. 'Looks like your little bookworm just wanted a quiet place to read!'

I looked where she was pointing. At the back of the room, curled up underneath a table, was Maisie! She had a book in her hand and was completely oblivious to her surroundings. She didn't even look up when Rebecca and I went into the room, and I had to bend right down under the table and say her name before she noticed me.

'Maisie! What are you doing here?'

Maisie looked up, wide-eyed and perfectly calm. 'Those boys were being so noisy. I needed somewhere quiet to read.'

I was too relieved to be cross, and I gave her a big hug. 'I'm glad you're all right. I think it's about time we headed home, don't you? You can find somewhere quiet to read there. Oh ...' I remembered about the books.

'What's wrong?' Rebecca asked.

'It's just we were all hoping to take out some books, but I don't have enough money to pay the fine first,' I said, blushing. 'For the book that got torn, you know – it wasn't Zach's fault ...'

'Don't worry about that,' Rebecca said. 'I know you'll pay it the next time you're in. Come with me and I'll check those books out for you.'

She led the way to the desk, completely ignoring Mr Jenkins, who was still grumbling, and checked out all our books. Bobby and Zach brought theirs over and Rebecca put those in the pile too. She handed them to me with a big smile. 'Now you're good to go – that should give you enough reading material for a few days!'

'Thanks so much,' I said. 'I'll have the money next time, I promise.'

I rounded the children up and headed for the door. I'd never felt so glad to be leaving the library before. But it had all ended a lot better than it could have. I shivered as I saw cars flying along the main road at top speed, and clutched Maisie's hand tightly. I was never letting her out of my sight again!

The library drama seemed to have had quite an effect on both the boys, who went off to their room to read their books without me even suggesting it. Maisie curled up on one end of the couch with hers, and I sat down with mine too. There was just time to read a bit more before I needed to start thinking about getting some lunch ready. Soon I was lost in the Fossils' world again, standing in the wings with Pauline feverishly going over Tyltyl's lines from *The Bluebird*, waiting for the cue to step onto the stage.

I made cheese and salad sandwiches for lunch, and cut up enough apples for everyone (Maisie and Bobby won't eat apples unless they're chopped up). I had just finished when Mum and Emma came through the door. Emma was cranky – she always gets like that when she's been out all morning and is late having her lunch.

'I'll take her, Mum,' I said, reaching out for my little sister.

'Thanks, Hannah.' Mum put her into my arms and went to call to the others.

I sang to Emma as I brought her over to her highchair, swaying her over and back in time to the song. She was smiling again by the time I handed her her own bread and cheese cut into easy-to-hold fingers.

Mum came back into the kitchen and planted a kiss on top of my head. 'Oh, Hannah, I don't know what I'd do without you. You're such a great big sister.'

Apart from losing Maisie, and letting Zach get into a row with Tyler, I thought to myself, feeling a bit guilty. But there was no point in worrying Mum now that it was all over so I just mumbled, 'Thanks' as I went to put the sandwiches on the table. I was glad to be finished with big sister duties for the day – and I'd definitely do a much better job the next time.

Chapter Eight

I squeezed through the gap in the hedge at exactly two minutes to three, the library copy of *Ballet Shoes* tucked under my arm. I found Meg spreading a picnic blanket on the lawn. 'I hope this is OK,' she said anxiously. 'We don't have any garden furniture yet.'

'Of course it is,' I said quickly. 'Although you should know that Ruby will probably turn it into an exercise mat and start doing her stretches on it.'

Meg laughed. 'She sure is obsessed with ballet, isn't she?'

There it was again — something in her voice that didn't sound Irish. Was it American maybe? I was about to comment, but Meg said, 'I think I hear the doorbell.'

She returned a minute later with Laura and Ruby.

'Hi, guys,' I said. 'Ready for another meeting of Star Club?'

'Definitely!' Ruby did a series of ballet leaps and landed on the rug beside me. 'Look, that was me being Posy showing her sisters a *pas de chat*. Oh.' She stopped and looked around. 'I'm not, like, assuming that I'm Posy or anything.

If anyone else wants to be her that's fine.' She lowered her eyes and started playing with the fringe on the rug.

'Yes, I was thinking I'd like to be Posy, actually,' Laura said, winking at me.

'Oh,' Ruby said, still not looking up.

'Yes, because I like joking around, just like Posy,' Laura said. 'Plus the fact that I'm so graceful, and so good at ballet, of the two-left-feet variety.' She couldn't keep it up any longer and suddenly burst out laughing. 'Ruby, you should see the look on your face!'

Ruby blushed. 'OK, you had me there! So I can be Posy then?' She looked from me to Meg, still a bit anxious.

'Of course you can,' I reassured her.

'You're perfect for it,' Meg added.

It was my turn to suddenly become very interested in Meg's rug instead of my friends' faces. 'Who does every-one else want to be?'

'I really don't mind,' Laura said. 'It depends what scenes we're going to do, really.'

'I'd quite like to be Petrova,' Meg said shyly. 'I really like her character. But I don't mind if you want to be her, Hannah.'

'I was hoping to be Pauline, actually,' I admitted.

'Looks like we're sorted, so!' Laura said. 'I'm happy to be whatever extra character is needed. I can do all sorts of parts – look.' She suddenly pulled a series of faces, from grumpy to miserable to over the moon with excitement, which had us all giggling once again.

We had all brought our copies of the book so we flicked through to scenes we thought we might do. We started reading bits out to each other, trying to get a feel for the characters we were playing.

We were just starting to get somewhere when I realised we had an audience. Maisie was watching us over the hedge.

'Maisie, what are you doing?' I demanded.

'Just watching,' Maisie said. 'Can I be in it? I could be the cousin who comes to visit.'

'There isn't a cousin,' I told her.

'Can I be the dog then? I'm really good at being a dog.' Maisie's head disappeared as she got down on all fours and started making barking noises through the hedge. Ruby collapsed into giggles.

'There isn't a dog either!' I told her, marching over to the hedge. 'Go away please, you're distracting us.'

Maisie stood up again. 'I don't have to go away. I'm only watching. It's a free country, isn't it?' I know she'd heard Zach saying the same thing to Bobby the day before and she'd obviously saved the remark to use later.

'Maisie!' I hissed at her. 'I mean it. Go away or I'm telling Mum.'

'Fine!' Maisie stomped off, shouting over her shoulder,

'It was pretty boring anyway, if you want to know!'

I went back over to my friends, feeling embarrassed. 'Sorry, guys. She can be a real pain sometimes.'

'She does make a pretty good dog,' Ruby giggled.

'We know where to turn if the plot takes an unexpected twist!' Meg said.

'Where were we?' I asked, wanting to drop the subject of Maisie. 'Laura, it was your turn I think.'

Laura was struggling a bit with the Russian accent for Madame Fidolia, the head of the theatre school the children were attending.

'Try watching videos of Russian people speaking on YouTube,' Meg suggested. 'It's a really handy way of practising accents.'

'That's a great idea, thanks,' Laura said.

'No problem. I used to do it all the time when ...' Meg stopped. 'When I was in a school play before. I had to play this French woman, and I just couldn't get the accent right. I ended up watching loads of clips of French actors speaking English until I was practically talking that way inside my head!'

She started demonstrating her French accent, accompanied by lots of dramatic hand gestures. I wondered what it was she had been about to say. One thing was for sure, it wasn't what she ended up saying.

My train of thought was interrupted by yelling from

next door as Bobby came charging into the garden swinging his lightsaber. Zach followed close behind him, wearing a Jedi knight mask and pointing a toy gun at him.

'You'll never get me!' Bobby shouted at him.

'Yes I will!' Zach shouted back. 'I've got supersonic blaster rays!'

I groaned. 'Sorry, guys.'

'Don't worry,' Laura said. 'We'll shut them up if they get too noisy. Let's go on with the next scene – I'll practise my Russian accent later.'

Meg and I started reading out some bits of dialogue between Pauline and Petrova, but I kept finding myself distracted by the *Star Wars* battle going on next door, especially when Zach apparently killed Bobby and he had to die with the loudest yells and groans you can imagine. Eventually though I managed to tune them out, and we had a fun afternoon, working out which scenes we'd do, and what parts we needed Laura to play.

I didn't even notice how much time had gone by until the doorbell started ringing. It was Ruby's brother coming to call her home for dinner. Ruby rushed off, promising to work out Posy's dance routine for next time.

Laura and I helped Meg to tidy up, then Laura said, 'I'd better be going too. Hannah, do you want to walk home with me?'

'I would but we're not exactly going in the same direction!' I pointed out.

'You're not in a hurry home though, are you?' Laura persisted.

'That's true.' Having listened to the boys' shouting coming over the hedge all afternoon, I definitely wasn't in a hurry to be back in the middle of that.

'Thanks for everything, Meg,' Laura said. 'We can go to my house next time.'

'See you then – and I'll definitely know my first set of lines,' Meg said with a smile as she opened the front door for us.

Laura waited until we were a little way down the road, then glanced back to check Meg had closed the door behind us. 'So, what do you think Meg's story is?'

'What do you mean?'

'There's something strange going on,' Laura said. 'She keeps starting to tell us things, and then clamming up. What's that about?'

'I'm not sure.' I knew exactly what Laura meant – I'd been thinking the same thing.

'I was asking her about her dad the other day, too, and she just changed the subject,' Laura went on.

'Oh, I don't really think you should have asked her that,' I said. 'She would tell us if she wanted to.'

I felt a bit protective of Meg. Even though she seemed pretty confident and outgoing, there was something a bit vulnerable about her, a sort of fragility that I couldn't quite explain.

Laura shrugged. 'I just don't see what the big deal is. If her parents have just split up then why not just tell us – I've been there, I could talk to her about it. Even if they split up ages ago and he's just not involved in her life, why not just say so – it doesn't have to be this deep dark secret.'

'Oh my God.' I stopped still. 'Laura – what if he's dead?'

Laura stopped too and looked at me in horror.

'What if he just died and they moved here for a fresh start? And she doesn't feel up to talking about him yet?'

Laura groaned. 'Oh God, I hope it's not that. Poor Meg, that would be just awful!'

'I know.'

'And not exactly helped by me asking her stupid questions.'

'I know! That's what I'm trying to say to you!'

Laura was looking so distraught that I tried to reassure her. 'It's probably not that. He's probably walking around somewhere, completely fine, and planning to visit any day now. It could be anything, really. I just think it's up to Meg how much she wants to tell us.'

'You're right,' Laura admitted. 'I'm just being nosey. Plus I'm convinced there's a good story there, and if you want to be a writer you have to always be on the lookout for stories!'

We'd reached the crossroads which is as far as I'm supposed to go. Laura was about to cross, but then she remembered. 'Oh, right. You're not allowed to come any further.'

I blushed. Even with my closest friend, who knows exactly what my mum is like, it was embarrassing. 'It's probably time to head home anyway, dinner will be ready.'

'What are you going to do for the meeting in my house?' Laura wanted to know.

'I'll think of something,' I muttered. Maybe Meg's mum could give us a lift – as long as Meg didn't mention Star Club. Or one of Ruby's parents. I'd figure something out.

As usual it took us about ten minutes to say goodbye. As I trudged off home, I thought again about what Laura had said. There was a mystery there all right, and the clues were pretty strange ones. And it wasn't all to do with her missing dad, either. Why didn't she talk about where they had lived before, and why did she have a slight accent that came out every now and again? What could be going on with Meg?

Chapter Nine

We'd arranged to have the next meeting of Star Club on Friday afternoon. I was hoping to see the other girls in between, but I was busy helping Mum, Ruby was busy with ballet, and Laura didn't even answer the phone when I called her. Meg didn't seem to be around either – when I had a bit of time to spare I sneaked into their garden through the hedge, but there was no sign of her when I peeped in the window.

I did as much as I could on my own though. I typed up the scene we'd worked out together and printed out copies for everyone. I learned all of Pauline's lines and practised putting in gestures too. The bedroom I shared with Maisie wasn't exactly ideal for rehearsing – I could only walk a few steps before banging into one of our beds, and that was after picking up all her toys from the floor – but I did my best. All the best artists have to suffer for their art, I told myself, picturing poets struggling to write in garret rooms in Paris, and wildlife photographers crouching in uncomfortable positions under bushes all day long in the hope of getting that one perfect shot. All I had to juggle with was a cramped bedroom and a noisy bunch of siblings.

By Friday I was really dying to see my friends again and have another rehearsal. I knew Mum wouldn't mind me spending the afternoon with my friends (I think I'd mentioned the rehearsal about seventeen times). It was looking like another crazy morning in our house though. I was sitting up in bed reading when Dad popped his head around the door. It wasn't even eight o'clock yet, but there was no chance of a lie-in with Maisie in the bed beside me singing to her teddies.

'Morning, girls,' Dad said. 'Hannah, Mum and Emma are still asleep. Emma kept us awake half the night, crying. She's teething again.' Dad had those dark circles under his eyes which he always gets when he's exhausted.

'Oh, poor Emma,' I said. 'And poor you too!'

'I know. I just hope I don't fall asleep in my meeting,' Dad said, running a hand through his hair and making it stand on end. 'Try to let Mum sleep if you can. She's worn out.'

'I'll take the others downstairs,' I told him, scrambling out of bed. 'It's a good thing Maisie didn't wake her with her singing!'

'I was using my morning singing voice,' Maisie said. 'It's quieter than my afternoon voice.'

'Thanks, Hannah,' Dad said. 'And well done on your lovely, quiet singing, Maisie. Bobby is already downstairs eating breakfast, and Zach's getting dressed. Just see if you can keep them occupied for an hour or two. I'd better get going.'

I got dressed quickly and took Maisie downstairs for breakfast, deciding it was easier to just leave her in her pyjamas for now. After breakfast I took out some arts and crafts stuff and helped Maisie and Bobby make houses out of shoe boxes. They made a huge mess but at least they were quiet. Zach was totally absorbed in his library book so he was no trouble.

It was ten o'clock by the time Mum came downstairs, looking bleary-eyed. 'She's teething,' Mum said, putting a rosy-cheeked Emma into her highchair. 'She'll be a lot better once this new tooth comes through.'

'I'll give her her breakfast,' I told Mum. 'You go and have a shower, you'll feel better then.'

'Thank you, Hannah, that would be great,' Mum said. 'But after that you should go out with your friends. You've been doing way more than your fair share around here this week, and you need some time off.'

I wasn't going to argue with that. Mum trudged back upstairs. I heated up some porridge for Emma, making sure it wasn't too hot. Giving Emma her breakfast is a complicated affair. It involves a little bit of spoonfeeding her the porridge when she'll let me (she'd rather just eat it with her hands) and quite a bit of stopping her from picking up the bowl and flinging it on the ground when she's had enough. Mum gives her those bowls with a rubber base that's meant to stick on to the highchair tray, but they are not much use against the determined force of Emma.

I'd just decided it was time to move on to toast when the doorbell rang.

'I'll get it!' shouted a voice from under the table. I hadn't even realised Maisie was in there.

'What are you doing?' I asked her.

'Feeding my teddies,' Maisie said. I looked under the table cloth and saw that she'd lined them up on a couple of chairs and had a bowl of cereal from which she was pretending to feed them. From the looks of things the teddies were being a lot more cooperative than Emma.

Maisie scrambled out and made for the door, but Zach was charging down the stairs.

'I said I was getting it!' Maisie roared at him.

'You're not allowed answer the door, you're too little,' Zach said.

'I am so allowed, if I check who it is first!' Maisie argued.

Emma had just about worked the bowl free. I snatched it away from her just in time. I really didn't need porridge everywhere. Emma let out a cry of protest.

The doorbell rang again.

'Well, SOMEONE answer it please!' I called.

I heard scuffles, but I was too busy trying to soothe Emma to go and investigate. Zach and Maisie came tumbling into the room, each of them complaining loudly about the other.

'Zach never lets me open the door!'

'Maisie's too little! She should let me do it!'

'OK, OK,' I said. 'Did one of you actually answer the door?'

'Eventually!' It was Meg, looking a little bit overwhelmed. 'Wow. I think I'll come through the hedge the next time,' she joked.

'Sorry,' I said. 'They always fight over answering the door.'

Zach went stomping off upstairs again. Maisie ran after him, still complaining.

I handed Emma a piece of toast. She stopped crying and quickly started gumming it.

'I just came over to see if you're free this morning,' Meg said. 'I'm going over to Sadie's house, and I thought you might like to come with me. She's got a great dressing-up box, and I thought we could have a look for some costumes for the show.'

'Oh, I'd love to,' I said. I glanced around the kitchen. It looked a little bit like a bomb had hit it. While I'd been occupied with Emma, Maisie had obviously brought her whole tea set in from the playroom to feed her teddies, dropping pieces here and there along the way. One half of the table was covered with arts and crafts stuff from earlier, and someone had spilled a bottle of glue on the floor and then run off and left it. All our breakfast dishes were still left by the sink, and open boxes of cereal and cartons of juice and milk sat on the other counter.

Meg followed my look. 'I'll help you clean up if you like,' she offered.

I sighed. 'Thanks Meg, that would be great. I should really make them all come and clean up after themselves, but it's more hassle than it's worth. Sometimes it's just easier to do it myself.'

Meg started loading the dishwasher, and I cleared up the art stuff. As I was mopping up the glue Maisie reappeared. 'Maisie, can you tidy up your tea set please?' I asked her.

'I'm still playing with it,' Maisie objected.

'Well, put it all together at least,' I said. 'People are going to step on it and break it the way it's all over the floor.'

Maisie grumbled a bit, but started picking up after herself.

Emma had finished her toast and was banging on her highchair tray with her spoon. She seemed happy enough so I left her where she was while I put away the breakfast things. I wiped down the counters with a cloth and looked around. 'Much better! Thanks for your help Meg.'

Hannah in the Spotlight

'No problem,' Meg said. 'So do you think you'll be allowed go?'

'I think so. I just need to wait until Mum's ready.' I heard the shower being switched off, so I knew she wouldn't be much longer.

The only thing that needed cleaning now was Emma. She'd managed to get porridge all over her babygro and even in her hair. I wet a facecloth under the tap and started cleaning her up, chatting to Meg all the while.

'I typed up that scene we were practising the last day so we could have a clean copy each. I know everyone had their own lines scribbled down, but I thought we'd need a proper copy.'

'Good idea, it's not much use in knowing your own lines if you don't know where they come in,' Meg said. 'I've been learning mine, but I'm not sure of all the cues.'

'I bet Ruby hasn't practised anything except her ballet steps,' I said, smiling.

I lifted Emma out of the highchair and sat her on my knee, playing clap handies with her.

Meg was watching me in fascination. 'I don't know how you do it,' she suddenly blurted out. 'I mean, how do you know how to do all this stuff? I wouldn't know where to start with a baby.'

I shrugged. 'I'm just used to it, I suppose. Maisie's nearly six now, but I used to help out with her when she was a baby too.'

Mum came into the kitchen. She looked much better after her shower, even though she hadn't bothered drying her hair properly.

'Oh, hi, Meg, nice to see you,' she said, self-consciously running a hand through her hair. She looked around the kitchen. 'I was about to apologise for the mess, but you've cleaned everything up, Hannah, you star!'

'Meg helped me,' I said.

'I had an ulterior motive,' Meg said with a grin. 'I'm hoping to steal Hannah away for the morning – would that be OK? We want to go to my granny's house to look at some costumes.'

'Sure,' Mum said, taking Emma from me. 'Where does your granny live?'

'She's over in Glencar, but Mum will give us a lift,' Meg explained. 'She's not starting her new job until Monday.'

'What time do you want me home?' I asked.

'Oh, there's no hurry,' Mum said. 'Take your time. We're going to have a quiet day here today, we've done enough rushing around lately. Just give me a ring if you're not going to be home for lunch.'

Bobby burst into the room. 'Hannah, can you help me find my Jedi mask? Zach says he didn't take it, but I know he did.'

'Hannah's going out,' Mum said firmly. 'I'll talk to Zach.'

She turned to me. 'Go on, go quickly before something else happens!'

I didn't need to be told twice. I grabbed my hoodie and my Star Club notebook, and Meg and I hurried out the door.

I closed the front door behind us. 'Freedom!' I tossed the notebook in the air and caught it again.

Meg giggled. 'Now we just need to get past my mum.'

'Oh, you haven't asked her?' I said in surprise.

'No, but it'll be fine. Just don't tell her why we're going to Sadie's, OK?'

Meg hopped over the wall and put her key in the front door. I followed her in. Cordelia was at the kitchen table, tapping away at her laptop, a mug of coffee beside her on the table. She looked up and smiled when we came in.

'Oh, darling, there you are,' she said. 'I'm just trying to figure out how to work this computer program. It's really quite confusing. I don't know why they have to make things so complicated these days.'

'Won't they give you training when you start next week?' Meg asked her.

Cordelia wrinkled up her nose. 'I may have told them I knew how to use it already. In fact, there's a chance I mentioned something about several years' experience.'

'Mum!' exclaimed Meg. 'You shouldn't lie about stuff like that!'

'Oh, it's just a teeny little lie,' Cordelia said. 'I desperately wanted the job you see.'

'What happens when they ask you to do something on Monday and you haven't a clue how it works?' Meg asked.

'I'll cross that bridge when I come to it,' Cordelia said breezily. 'I'm sure a quick crash course today will bring me right up to speed. What are you two up to today, anyway? No dramatics I hope?' She laughed.

'No, we're just hanging out,' Meg said quickly. 'Actually, I said I'd go over to Sadie's this morning, and Hannah's going to come with me. Could you give us a lift?'

'Sure. I need a break from this dreary old swotting anyway,' Cordelia said.

She stood up and drained the last of her coffee, then reached for her car keys and headed for the door.

I couldn't help thinking how different things were for Meg, being an only child. If I asked Mum for a lift somewhere, I'd get the third degree about why I needed to go, and then even if she did say she'd bring me we'd have to get all the others into the car too, and that would most likely involve feeding Emma first and changing her nappy and waiting for the bigger three to find all the toys and books they couldn't possibly manage without for a short car trip. Meg just had to ask her mum, and a minute later we were getting into the car.

I got into the back seat and Meg sat up front beside her mum.

'I'll probably spend most of the day on the computer, so why don't you see if Sadie can keep you for lunch?' Cordelia suggested as we pulled out of the drive.

'OK, I will. And then maybe we can call over to Laura's afterwards, she lives just across the road from Sadie.'

Meg caught my eye in the rearview mirror and gave me a teeny smile. Clearly this had been her plan all along. I smiled back. Meg was a pretty good person to have on my team.

Chapter Ten

Sadie's attic was like something from a film. It was crammed full with all sorts of everything, but it wasn't the normal sort of clutter and half-broken stuff most attics were filled with. A stunning Tiffany lamp, the kind with colourful stained glass, stood on top of a mahogany bookcase, whose shelves were filled with stacks of what looked like manuscripts. A gorgeous old-fashioned bike with a wicker basket leaned against one side, and beside it lay a big black telephone, the kind with a separate piece to speak into and a trumpet-shaped piece to hold to your ear. A pile of old curtains lay on top of a throne encrusted with jewels.

'Oh my God. This is amazing!' I managed to say. Already I was picturing all the scenes we could act out with these fabulous props. The bike made me think of *The Wizard of Oz*, and the phone was just like the one in *It's a Wonderful Life*. The throne would be perfect for any fairytale, and the curtains could be used for so many different things.

'You haven't even seen the best bit yet,' Meg said. 'Give me a hand with this, will you?'

She indicated a huge brown trunk with leather handles, which lay underneath a scratched folding table. I took one of the handles and together we pulled it out to where there was more space.

Meg took down a key that was hanging from a chain on a nail above our heads, and inserted it in the lock. I was half expecting to see gold coins and sparkling tiaras, but what was inside was even better.

'Oh my God. Costumes!'

The trunk was stuffed full with theatrical clothing of all sorts.

'Look at this!' I found an amazing feather boa, long and thick and deep pink. I flung it around my neck and modelled it for Meg.

'You need this to go with it,' Meg said, plonking a floppy hat with a feather in it on my head. 'And this!' She handed me a huge sparkly shoulder bag.

A full-length mirror stood under the dormer window. I walked over to it, admiring my reflection in the dim light from the bare bulb overhead.

Meg came to join me, wearing a full-length ballgown in royal blue and a long string of beads.

'Well, we don't look much like Pauline and Petrova, but we do look pretty good,' she giggled.

I was so engrossed in the amazing costumes I'd actually forgotten what we were supposed to be looking for.

'Where did Sadie get all this stuff?' I asked. 'It's so cool.'
I rummaged through the trunk again and pulled out some
more hats – a top hat, slightly out of shape, but still smart,
a soldier's helmet and an Easter bonnet.

'Oh, she just likes collecting old stuff,' Meg said. 'Look,
this is her wedding dress, can you believe it?' She showed
me a beautiful lace dress with long sleeves and little pearls
sewn in around the neckline. It was a bit old-fashioned,
but still so elegant. Meg held it up against her and went
over to the mirror once more.

'How are you getting on up there?' Sadie called from
the bottom of the steps.

'Great. Look what I found,' Meg said, leaning over the
open hatch with the wedding dress.

'Be careful!' Sadie said quickly. 'I don't want you falling. What have you got there? Oh, my beautiful wedding
dress! I did hope your mum would wear it for her wedding, but she wanted something a bit more modern.'

'I can't picture Mum in this,' Meg agreed. 'Maybe I'll
wear it some day!'

'I hope you do,' Sadie said. 'Well, let me know if you
need any help.'

I heard the patter of her footsteps as she went back
downstairs. Meg folded the wedding dress carefully and
put it to one side.

'Sadie's so nice,' I said to her. 'You must be glad to be

living near her again.'

'Oh yes, it's great,' Meg said. 'It's the best thing about — well, everything. Oh, look! I knew there was something like this here.' She pulled out a dark green gingham dress, a bit like an old-fashioned school uniform. 'Look, don't you think this would do for one of the girls?' She held it up against her.

'It's perfect!' I said. 'Wow, it's so great to be able to use all this stuff.'

'Let's see what else there is.'

We rummaged through the rest of the clothes and found a couple of other things we thought might work — a simple jumper and a kilt for one of the girls, a long sweeping black skirt for Madame Fidolia, and a tweed skirt and high-collared white blouse for Nana.

'Lucky Laura gets to have the most fun with her costumes,' Meg said. 'She's going to love all this stuff. Do you think we need anything for Ruby, or will she just wear her normal ballet gear?'

'We'd better find her a jumper and skirt as well if we can,' I said. 'Posy wouldn't be wearing her ballet gear on the first day, when they go to the academy.'

'Oh, good point,' Meg said. 'Let's see what else we can find.'

We tried on one thing after another and modelled them for each other, striding up and down the attic as if we were on the catwalk.

'Meg! Hannah!' Sadie called. 'Lunch is ready whenever you want to come down!'

'Good, I'm hungry after all this hard work,' Meg said with a giggle.

We gathered up all the clothes and accessories we thought we might use, then Meg shoved the rest back into the trunk. I went down the ladder first and Meg threw everything down to me one by one.

'Stand back, this is a big one!' she shouted.

I quickly stepped back into the bathroom, just in time to dodge an enormous book which Meg flung down the ladder. It fell on the landing with a giant thud, and I saw that it was the *Complete Works of Shakespeare*. No wonder it had made such a noise!

'Oops,' said Meg. 'Just thought that might come in handy.'

'Everything OK up there?' Sadie called up the stairs.

'Yes thanks!' Meg said.

'That's good, because it sounds a bit like a herd of elephants is about to fall through my ceiling,' Sadie said. 'Did you find what you were looking for?'

'We got tons of brilliant stuff,' I told her. 'Are you sure you don't mind us borrowing it?'

'Of course not,' Sadie said. 'It's lovely to see it being used again.'

'We'll take good care of it, I promise,' I said, following Sadie and Meg into the kitchen. 'Where did you get it all?'

'Oh, I'm sure Meg's told you all about how I used to—'

'How you used to go around all the vintage markets collecting things,' Meg interrupted. 'Yes, I was just starting to tell you, Hannah.'

An odd look passed between Sadie and Meg before Sadie turned away to the hob, where a big saucepan full of soup was bubbling away. 'Yes, that's right. I've always liked collecting things. And there are some wonderful markets around. Meg sometimes comes with me – you can come with us some day too if you like.'

She handed me a steaming bowl of soup, then went back to ladle out some more for Meg and herself.

'I'd love to,' I said. I glanced at Meg, but she wouldn't meet my eye. Somehow the atmosphere had changed in the room.

'What are you girls up to later?' Sadie asked, putting a big basket of bread down on the table.

'We're going over to Laura's to rehearse,' Meg said. 'But don't tell Mum, OK?'

Sadie frowned. 'Why not?'

'She's just being a bit funny about the whole thing,' Meg said, reaching for a piece of bread. 'Don't worry, Sadie. I'm not lying to her or anything. I'm just choosing not to pass on particular information unless absolutely necessary.'

Meg was good at that, I thought to myself.

Sadie muttered something that sounded a bit like 'What a lot of secrets'.

Meg started telling Sadie all about the scenes we'd been doing. Sadie was so enthusiastic that Meg got up and started acting out her part. She was word-perfect already, I was thrilled to see. I'd been a bit worried that I'd end up having to convince everyone to learn their lines, but that definitely wasn't going to be the case with Meg. More than that, I already got the sense that she *was* Petrova. When she was acting out the scene where Petrova is rehearsing for a part in a play and getting everything wrong she seemed to have captured Petrova just right – her reluctance to act at all, but also her worry about making a fool of herself.

'Wonderful, Meg!' Sadie said. 'You're doing a very good job of showing us how Petrova feels in this scene. How about you, Hannah? Show me what you've been rehearsing.'

I suddenly felt very shy, but I made myself get up and join in. If I couldn't act in front of Meg's lovely granny, how would I ever stand up in front of an audience?

We decided to act out the scene where Pauline needs a new dress to go to an audition. Her old velvet dress was shabby and worn and too short for her, but they had no money for a new one. It was one of my favourite parts of the book, because the girls are all so anxious that Pauline has to look right for her audition, and so determined to find a way around their money troubles.

When we had finished I turned nervously to Sadie, hoping she'd have something encouraging to say, but she had her head on one side and was frowning a little, as if she was thinking deeply. Meg wasn't saying anything either.

The silence was too much for me, and I blurted out, 'Well, what did you think?'

'Well, you certainly know your lines, and you've got the pauses in the right places, and the gestures too,' Sadie said. 'But tell me, Hannah, what were you feeling when you were speaking?'

'What do you mean?' I asked.

'What was going through your head? Where were you picturing yourself?'

'I'm not sure,' I admitted. 'I was just concentrating on getting my lines right.'

'I thought so. Because I have to tell you, I didn't get the sense that I was watching Pauline speaking, feeling worried about making a good impression at her audition, anxious about how they'll pay for a new dress, but also feeling proud of the fact that she's old enough to get an acting licence and might be earning money for the family. All I saw was Hannah, who's learned all her lines perfectly, it's true, but who's never known what it's like to feel worried about money, and who's never worn a velvet dress, shabby or otherwise!'

I could feel my face burning. How could Sadie think I wasn't convincing as Pauline? I *loved* Pauline – she was my favourite character – I'd wanted to be her from the minute Ruby suggested doing *Ballet Shoes*. I *did* know how she felt – I might not have worn a velvet dress, or travelled to theatre school on the London Underground, but I had the same longing to be on the stage that she had, the same passion for taking on a new role.

But as Sadie went on the realisation crept over me that she was right. My annoyance started to turn to embarrassment. I'd been so busy being the Star Club director that I'd forgotten to work hard enough on my own acting.

Sadie seemed to know how I was feeling, and she patted me gently on the shoulder. 'Now don't be disheartened, Hannah. You have plenty of potential, I can see that already. You just need to practise getting inside your character's mind. For example, how do you think Pauline feels when Petrova suggests selling their necklaces to earn money to buy the new dress? Think about it for a minute before you answer.'

Meg was pretending to be deeply engrossed in the script, which I was grateful for. I thought for a minute like Sadie said, then I said hesitatingly, 'She's excited that they have a plan and that she'll be able to get a new dress and not have to go to the audition in her ordinary clothes like

Nana was suggesting. But she feels guilty that Petrova and Posy have to sell their necklaces too. She's all mixed up.'

'Exactly!' Sadie exclaimed. 'You *do* understand her! You just need to really think about it while you're speaking so you can convey those feelings in your voice and in your movements. Now, let's run through it again.'

I did my best to ignore my embarrassment and throw myself into the character of Pauline. Sadie made us go over the lines again and again, and suddenly I felt something click. I knew from Sadie's reaction when I said the line, 'If only we had some money', that I'd finally got it right, though she didn't say anything until we'd got to the end of the scene.

'Fantastic, girls!' she exclaimed then. 'Hannah, that's much better. Keep working on that and you'll get there in no time.'

'Thanks, Sadie,' I said.

'Look at the time!' Meg exclaimed. 'We need to get to Laura's.'

'I was supposed to ring my mum,' I remembered. 'Could I use the phone, Sadie?'

'Of course.' Sadie tapped her password into her mobile and handed it to me.

I tried phoning Mum, but there was no answer, so I sent her a text instead. 'Going to Laura's for rehearsal. Will get lift home with Meg. Hannah.'

It would be so much easier if she would just let me have my own phone, I thought yet again.

As I went to hand the phone back to Sadie, her screen-saver popped up. It was a photo of Meg and her mum with a smiling, dark-haired man.

Meg saw me looking, but all she said was, 'Can you grab those costumes, Hannah? I'll carry the book.'

'Be careful with it,' Sadie said. 'That's your grandad's, and he still uses it for reference sometimes.'

Meg looked a bit guilty and whispered to me, 'Just as well he didn't see me flinging it out of the attic then.'

As we were leaving I paused to say goodbye to Sadie. 'Thanks, Sadie. You've been a great help.'

Sadie smiled at me. 'Any time. I can't wait to see how your show turns out.'

Chapter Eleven

Laura's house was across the road, just a few doors down. We rang the doorbell for ages before her sister Andrea came to answer it. 'Hi girls, are you looking for Laura?'

'Yes, she should be expecting us,' I said.

'Come on in,' Andrea said. 'Laura didn't mention anything, but then I've hardly seen her the last few days. She's writing a new story.'

I groaned. 'So that's why she wasn't answering the phone. She's probably totally forgotten about our rehearsal.' I turned to Meg. 'When Laura starts a new story she gets completely absorbed in it and the rest of the world might as well not exist.'

'You can go on up to her room,' Andrea told us. 'You might have better luck getting her attention than I've had. When I went to call her for lunch, she just grunted at me, so I left her to it. Her sandwich is still sitting on the kitchen counter.'

I hung the pile of costumes over the banisters and ran up the stairs to Laura's room, Meg following behind me. I knocked on the door and poked my head around.

Despite the brightness of the day the curtains were tightly shut, and the lamp at Laura's desk was switched on, the only light in the room. She was hunched over it, surrounded by piles of paper, which seemed to be covered in her sprawling handwriting. More paper was scattered on the floor around her and on her unmade bed.

'I told you, Andrea, I don't want any breakfast,' Laura said, not looking up from her desk.

'It's not Andrea, it's us,' I told her. 'And it's after lunchtime!'

'Oh!' Laura jumped to her feet, nearly knocking over a half-drunk cup of tea. She turned the paper she had been writing on face down.

'What are you writing?' Meg asked. She picked up one of the sheets of paper from the floor. Laura practically snatched it out of her hand.

Meg looked a bit shocked, and even I was surprised. I know from experience that Laura NEVER lets anyone see what she's writing until she's finished, but it wasn't like her to be quite so jumpy.

'It's just a story,' Laura said. She ushered us towards the door. 'Sorry, guys, I totally forgot we were supposed to be having a rehearsal. Come on, we can go down to the sitting room.'

She closed the bedroom door firmly behind her and waited until we'd started going down the stairs before coming after us.

'Do you want a cup of tea?' Laura asked when we got to the kitchen; she was suddenly smiley and normal again. 'Actually, I think I might get some toast. I don't seem to have had any breakfast.'

'Or lunch,' I reminded her. 'Andrea said she left a sandwich for you. We had lunch in Meg's granny's house, but tea would be great.'

Laura eyed the sandwich on the counter with distaste. The bread looked all dry and the edges had started to curl. 'She should have told me she'd made me lunch.'

Meg and I exchanged a grin as Laura tipped the sandwich into the bin and put on some toast instead.

'Wait till you see the great costumes we found,' Meg said. She went to retrieve them from the hall, and came in modelling the green gingham dress.

'Oh, that's brilliant!' Laura said. She reached for the long black skirt. 'Is this for Madame Fidolia? It's perfect.' She pulled it on over her jeans and started striding around the kitchen, proclaiming, 'Marvellous, children!' She declared that she felt more Russian already.

The doorbell rang and Ruby rushed in, full of apologies for being late. 'Sorry – ballet camp ran over, then I had to get some lunch.'

'That's OK, we're a little behind schedule here too,' I told her as Laura started to spread peanut butter on her mountain of toast.

We finally got down to some rehearsing once Laura had devoured her toast and the rest of us had drunk several cups of tea. It was amazing how wearing our costumes really helped us get into character. Wearing the old-fashioned kilt and brown jumper we'd chosen for Pauline helped me to feel more like her, and with all the advice Sadie had given me running through my head I found it easier to stop being Hannah and start being Pauline. And Laura was much more convincing as Madame Fidolia in her long black skirt – it seemed to make her move more like a grown-up lady than a twelve-year-old girl. By the time Meg's mum came to collect us, I felt like we were really getting somewhere.

'My house on Monday?' I suggested as we gathered up our stuff.

'It's a date!'

'So when are we going to see this show of yours?' Dad asked.

I had my parents all to myself for once – the others were all, finally, in bed. I get to stay up an hour later than Zach and Bobby because I'm older, but usually by the time they're all in bed and the dinner dishes are done, Mum and Dad are so exhausted they just collapse in front of the TV. This evening the sun was still shining so the three of us were sitting in the back garden having a cup of tea.

'I've been hearing all about it from Mum – it sounds like you've been putting a lot of work into it,' Dad went on.

'Yes, we have,' I said. 'We're not ready to show anyone just yet though. Maybe in a few weeks.'

'I think you need to set a goal for yourselves,' Dad said. 'Otherwise it can be hard to stay focused.'

'We could do something for the end of the holidays maybe,' I said.

'Oh, I know!' Mum said. 'You can be the entertainment for Maisie's birthday party!'

I stared at her.

'It'd be perfect,' Mum enthused. 'We can have it here in the garden, and all Maisie's friends can come and watch. Then we can give them pizza and birthday cake and we're done – perfect party!'

'Sounds like a great plan,' Dad said. 'And less likely to result in broken bones than a bouncy castle.'

'Cheaper than a magician,' Mum added.

'Less mess than a paddling pool party,' said Dad.

'And much less stress than Pass the Parcel and Musical Chairs,' Mum finished.

They looked extremely happy with their little plan.

'What do you think, Hannah?' Mum asked at last.

'Ummm ... we could, I suppose ...' I said slowly. 'We're

going to need a LOT more rehearsals first though.'

'Have as many as you like!' Dad said. 'Believe me, it'll all start to come together quickly when you have a date to aim for.'

I started to feel a bit excited. They might only be a gang of six-year-olds, but it would still be our first proper audience. I pictured a big gang of them sitting on the grass, and my friends and I on the raised patio area, which would make a perfect stage. The only question was, could we do it on time? Maisie's birthday was only three weeks away. And even though our rehearsal that day had gone well, I knew we needed a lot more practice. Sadie had inspired me to strive to give the best performance I could, and it would take plenty of work to be truly convincing as Pauline.

'I'll have to call a club meeting,' I said. 'We need to discuss it together. I'll get back to you once I've consulted with the rest of the club.'

'Of course,' said Dad.

'Very important,' said Mum.

'We certainly wouldn't want to stand in the way of the democratic process,' said Dad.

'Or the rehearsals,' said Mum. 'You let me know when you need the garden, and I'll make sure the other four are occupied.'

'Thank you, Mum,' I said. 'That would be great.'

'And you'll have to look after all the organisation your-self, Hannah,' Dad added. 'Organising props or ...' he waved his hand as if he didn't know quite how to describe all the work involved in putting on a show, 'whatever. I'm going to be away in China that week on a business trip, so Mum will be busy.'

'Busier, you mean,' Mum murmured. 'I can't remember the last time I wasn't busy.'

'Of course I will,' I said. 'I would have done that anyway. The whole club will help. I can't wait to talk to them. I'll just pop over and see if Meg can come over tomorrow.'

I only remembered when I was slipping through the hedge that Dad didn't know about our secret passage – oops – I'd probably get a lecture on damaging the hedge when I got back.

As I got near to the back door, I heard Meg talking and realised she was on the phone. She sounded kind of agitated. 'Dad, can we not talk about this now? You know Mum doesn't want me to ... I know ... I know ... Look, Dad, I think we'd better drop it, OK? Do you want to talk to Mum? Dad, are you still there?'

Meg sounded so different – more stressed than I'd ever seen her, but also more grown up. My first thought was relief that her dad was indeed alive and well, but I wondered what on earth it was that they couldn't talk about. Then I realised I shouldn't be listening in on a private conversation, and I backed away as quickly as I could.

'Back already?' Mum asked.

'Yes – Meg's, um, I think she's busy,' I said. 'Can I ring Laura instead?'

'Is it a bit late to be ringing?' Dad wondered, checking his watch.

'Not Laura,' I said. 'There aren't any younger ones in her house.'

'OK, go ahead,' Dad told me.

'Thanks!' I jumped up and grabbed the phone from the kitchen, taking it into the playroom so I could have a bit more privacy.

'Laura? It's me, Hannah.'

'Oh, hi! I was just going to ring you actually. I need to talk to you – can we meet up tomorrow?'

'That's what I was going to ask you!' I told her. 'Do you want to come over to my house tomorrow afternoon? I'll let Ruby and Meg know in the morning.'

'OK, but I wanted to talk to you – just the two of us – first,' Laura said. 'Can you meet me at the library in the morning? Say ten o'clock?'

'Sure,' I said. 'What's it about?'

'I've got a new theory. I don't want to talk about it over the phone.'

Trust Laura to think someone was bugging our phones, I thought.

'Come on your own, OK?' Laura went on. 'And don't tell anyone else.'

Now she was really sounding like someone with a mad conspiracy theory. I decided to indulge her. 'OK Laura, I'll be there.'

'See you then!'

Laura hung up.

What could all that be about, I wondered? It felt like there were an awful lot of mysteries about at the moment.

Chapter Twelve

'OK, I've got a new theory,' Laura told me.

We were sitting on the wall outside the library, swinging our legs. I'd checked to see who was behind the desk, and sure enough it was the grumpy old Mr Jenkins. He certainly wouldn't let us away with talking in the library, even in whispers, so we'd just have to have our little chat outside.

'About what?'

'About the Mystery of Meg, of course,' Laura said.

I rolled my eyes. 'Not that again.'

Laura was unperturbed. 'Now you're going to think this is crazy, but just listen to me. It all adds up when you think about it.'

'WHAT does? Laura, you're not making any sense.'

'OK, here goes.' Laura paused for dramatic effect. 'Meg and her mother are on the run. Her parents are locked in a custody dispute over her, and her mum has run away with her so her dad can't have her.'

Laura sat back and waited for my reaction. I stared at her

incredulously. 'You can't be serious, Laura.'

'Think about it!' Laura said. 'It all makes perfect sense!' She began ticking the points off on her fingers. 'She won't talk about her dad at all. She won't say anything about whether her parents are divorced. She never mentions any plans to go to see him.'

'That hardly means her mum has kidnapped her!' I said.

Laura ignored me. 'She doesn't have a mobile phone, even though up until now I thought you and Ruby were the only twelve-year-olds in the western world who didn't have one. That's so her dad can't track her down using the signal. Private investigators can trace people using all that sort of stuff.'

I rolled my eyes again. Then I thought of the conversation I'd overheard the night before. I was about to say something, but Laura continued unabated. 'She sometimes uses American words for things, like she said "sidewalk" instead of "footpath" the other day, and "chips" instead of "crisps", and sometimes she has a bit of an American accent. But she's never said she used to live in America when we asked her where they lived before.'

'That's true,' I had to admit. 'But it hardly means she's been kidnapped.'

'Think about it,' Laura insisted. 'They have a different legal system over there. Say her dad's an American citizen, and her mum is Irish, which we know she is. Say they're divorcing. There's no way the courts would let Meg's mum take her out of the country. So she had no choice but to run away with her if she wanted to come home.'

'Yes, but …' I seized on a fatal flaw in Laura's theory. 'Meg's mum comes from Carrickbeg. Surely this is the first place her dad would come to look for them if they'd run away.'

'I thought about that,' Laura said. 'But they haven't moved in with Meg's granny. You said she had tons of room in her house, so why haven't they moved in there?'

I waited. No doubt Laura would have a rational explanation.

'So they have an early warning system!' Laura said. 'If he comes looking for them there, Meg's granny can warn her mum, and she'll have time to take off for somewhere else. Living next door to you means they have the best of both worlds. They can be near to Meg's granny, and all her mum's friends, but they'll know in advance if he's trying to track them down.'

I was still sceptical. 'I don't know, Laura. It seems to me that if they were really on the run they'd have chosen somewhere brand new, where they have no connections.'

'Well, there's also the fact that if he DID track them down Meg's mum would be protected by the Irish courts,' Laura argued. 'Meg is an Irish citizen, so she couldn't be sent back to the States if the custody case was held here.'

'I suppose ...' I didn't want to admit it, but Laura's theory was starting to sound a little bit plausible.

Laura had saved the best for last. 'Final point,' she said. 'Why did Meg's mother not want her to be in Star Club? She's a really laidback mum, it seems like she lets Meg do pretty much what she wants.'

'I don't know, I can't figure that one out at all,' I said.

'Because she might be in a show,' Laura said. 'She could get her picture in the local paper, and they're all online now, so if her dad was searching for her he'd know exactly where she was. Now do you see?'

'You know, you might actually be on to something,' I said slowly.

Laura stared at me. 'Oh my God! I didn't really believe it until you said that!'

'What?'

'I thought it was just me being crazy, but now that you've said it I'm thinking it's almost definitely true! Oh my God! Poor Meg!'

'Laura, wait a minute—'

'No, you're right, Hannah. There's definitely something in it. No wonder Meg is so jumpy all the time! It's like something out of a spy story.'

A thought struck me. 'Is that what you've been writing about? Meg's family?'

Laura looked a bit guilty.

'It is, isn't it?' I said. 'That's why you didn't want her seeing your story yesterday.'

Laura scratched at the ground with the toe of her shoe, not looking at me. 'I may have been inspired by real-life events in some of my writing this week.'

'Oh, Laura, I don't think that's very fair,' I said. 'Meg is our friend.'

'Well, it's not like I'm going to show the story to anyone,' Laura argued. 'I'm just writing it for me, really. You know what I'm like — I'm seized with an idea and I just have to write about it. Anyway, my story's not the important thing. The important thing is, what are we going to do?'

'What are we going to do about what?' I was having trouble keeping up with Laura's train of thought.

'About Meg, of course! If she really has been kidnapped.'

'What can we do?' I said. 'It's nothing to do with us. Meg and her mum seem perfectly happy. We don't even know if there's anything in your theory, you might have got it totally wrong.'

'Well, just pretend for a minute that I'm right. What should we do?'

I thought for a minute. 'Still nothing, except be there for Meg if she needs us. And I guess we should keep an eye out for anything strange, and look after her as much as we can.'

'And keep our eyes and ears open for any clues,' Laura

said. 'You never know when something will come along.'

'Are you two going to sit on the wall there all day?' It was a grumpy-looking Mr Jenkins, standing in the library door glowering at us. 'You're putting the paying customers off.'

'It's a library. No one has to pay to use it,' Laura pointed out. I didn't know how she dared to speak to him like that.

'Yes, it's a library. Not a teenage hang-out joint,' Mr Jenkins snapped. 'So either come in or go home. You're not sitting on that wall a minute longer, not if I have anything to do with it.'

I hopped down from the wall. It really wasn't worth arguing with Mr Jenkins when he was like this. Laura followed me more slowly. Mr Jenkins waited until we were walking down the road before storming back inside.

'Such a charming man,' Laura said. 'His wife is a very lucky lady.'

'God, do you think he's married?' I giggled. 'Who would marry him?'

'Only someone who needs their head examined!'

'I'd better get home,' I said. 'I promised Mum I wouldn't be long, and Maisie wants me to help her with an art project. I'd better get it done now so I'll be free for our meeting this afternoon.'

'I'm going to go into town,' Laura said. 'I want to get some hair stuff for putting my hair into a bun. For when

I'm Madame Fidolia, you know.'

'See you later then!'

'Yep.' Laura got on her bike. 'Don't forget to keep an eye on Meg's house, and give me a ring if you spot anything unusual.'

I watched her cycle off. Laura was always so dramatic. There couldn't really be any truth in her theory about Meg – could there?

Chapter Thirteen

Maisie's art project kept me busy for the rest of the morning.

'What is it you want to make, Maisie?' I asked her when I got home.

'A massive, ginormous banner,' Maisie informed me, 'saying "Happy Birthday, Maisie".'

I bit my lip, trying not to laugh. 'Isn't that the sort of thing you make for someone else as a surprise? Not for yourself, I mean.'

Maisie frowned at me. 'Why not?'

'Well, you don't say "happy birthday" to yourself, do you?' I pointed out.

'*I* do,' Maisie said. 'When I wake up on my birthday, I always say "Happy birthday, Maisie", even before I get out of bed.'

'OK. But what about Mum's birthday banner? She probably wants to use that.'

Mum's birthday banner was beautiful – bunting in all the colours of the rainbow, with HAPPY BIRTHDAY spelled out, one letter on each triangle. She'd made it herself, every bit of it stitched by hand, for my first birthday. That was when she only had one child, and a lot more time on her hands.

Maisie was dismissive. 'That's *your* birthday banner. I want one of my own.'

'It belongs to everyone now,' I said. 'I know Mum made it for me, but it doesn't say "Hannah" on it, and Mum puts it up for everyone's birthday.'

Maisie shrugged. 'She can still put it up if she wants. Just somewhere less important, like maybe the kitchen. Mine is going to go in the garden, where the party is. And it's going to say "Happy Birthday *Maisie*" on it, so everyone knows it's just mine.'

Maisie had that determined look on her face that I knew meant she would keep on arguing until she wore me down. Suddenly I saw where she was coming from. Almost all her clothes were hand-me-downs from me, packed away in bin bags and stored in the attic when I outgrew them, to be taken down a few years later for Maisie. A lot of her toys were the same. Her scooter was the one Zach had outgrown, and her bike had once been Bobby's. And since Emma had come along Maisie wasn't even the baby of the family any more, and she got much less of Mum's time. Maisie's birthday was the only thing that was just hers.

'OK, Maisie,' I said. 'You go and get the paints out, and I'll find some paper. Do you want coloured paper or white?'

'White,' Maisie called over her shoulder as she went off in search of the paints. 'I'm going to be using lots and lots of glitter.'

I was a bit nervous that afternoon as I told the other girls what Mum had suggested. Would they think we weren't ready to put on our show yet? Or would they think a six-year-old's birthday party was a strange place to be putting on our first show?

I needn't have worried, though. Everyone liked the idea right away.

'It's great to have something to aim for,' Meg said. 'And three weeks is lots of time to rehearse, we should be perfect by then!'

'Or good enough for six-year-olds, anyway,' Ruby giggled. 'I'm glad our first audience is going to be young! I was a bit scared someone was going to suggest doing it when we go back to school or something. The thoughts of performing in front of our whole class!'

'You've performed in front of hundreds of people before,' Laura pointed out.

'Yes but that was dancing,' Ruby said. 'My body just takes over. Acting is different. I'm not inside the music, I'm still there in my own head.'

When Ruby got onto the subject of ballet it was sometimes like she was talking a foreign language.

'So everyone's OK with the idea?' I asked, still a little anxious.

'Yes, stop worrying!' Laura said. 'It sounds great. Maisie will love it.'

'Cool.' I opened my star-covered notebook. 'OK, we really need to start planning then! We'll have to have a regular schedule for rehearsals, and make up our minds for certain about what scenes we're doing, and what costumes we'll need, and who's going to look after the props ...'

'How was your meeting?' Mum asked, after I got home.

'Great,' I told her. 'Everyone's on board.'

'Glad to hear it!' Mum said. 'I guess it's time to tell Maisie the news about the party then.'

'News about the party? My party? What's the news? How come Hannah knows and not me?' Maisie had appeared behind Mum and was practically jumping up and down on the spot with excitement.

I pretended to think hard. 'News? Was there news, Mum?'

'Do you know, I think I've forgotten what it is,' Mum said. 'Was it that we're going to have krispie buns?'

'That's not news. We always have krispie buns!' Maisie said.

'Was it that Maisie gets to wear her party dress?' I wondered.

'I *always* wear my party dress,' Maisie said. Now she actually *was* jumping up and down. 'Stop being silly! Tell me, tell me, tell me!'

Mum grinned. 'Oh, all right then. It's about the party entertainment.'

'There's going to be entertainment?' Maisie squealed.

'A brand new and very exclusive type of entertainment,' I told her. 'In fact, this theatre group is going to put on their very first show just for you.'

'Star Club?' Maisie exclaimed. 'Just for my party, really? All of you?'

'Yes, all of us. We're going to practise really hard to make your birthday show perfect.'

'Oh wow, oh wow, oh wow!' Maisie hugged me around the waist, then ran around the table to do the same thing to Mum. 'So can I be the dog then?'

Oh no – it looked like Maisie had got the wrong idea. 'No, Maisie, I told you, there isn't a dog.'

'Is there a cat?' Maisie dropped down on to all fours and started rubbing her side along Mum's legs in what I had to admit was a pretty good impression of a cat.

'There aren't any animals,' I said. I looked at Mum for help.

'Maisie, I'm not sure you understand,' Mum said gently.

'It's Hannah and her friends who are going to be in the show. You're going to be in the audience. The most important person in the audience,' she added hastily, seeing Maisie's face.

'What do you mean I'm not in the show?' Maisie said. 'It's my party, isn't it? Can't I even have a teeny tiny part?'

'Well ...' Mum raised her eyebrows at me.

'No!' I said. 'Sorry, Maisie, but it's a Star Club show, and we have it all planned out. I can't just go adding more people to it. It wouldn't be fair.'

'But it ISN'T fair!' Maisie said. 'It's supposed to be MY party!' She went stomping out of the room.

Mum sighed. 'Oh dear, I thought she'd love the idea. I don't suppose you could give her some small part, Hannah? She's so interested in your show, and it is her birthday.'

'No, Mum!' I felt like stomping out of the room myself. 'Sorry, but this is my thing with my friends. I don't want Maisie taking over.'

Mum ruffled my hair. 'Fair enough. I'll talk to Maisie, I'm sure she'll come round.'

I watched Mum walking away, feeling a bit guilty. I knew Maisie would love to be in the show – but honestly, couldn't I have one thing where I had a break from being a big sister?

Chapter Fourteen

The next two weeks went by in a bit of a whirlwind of rehearsals, organising props, finding costumes and practising hairstyles.

Maisie came to watch us rehearse, and although she was enchanted by Ruby's ballet dancing, and laughed at the row between the sisters, there were a couple of other parts where she seemed kind of distracted. All right, if I'm honest, she seemed a little bored. I started to feel worried. Was it just because she had seen it too many times by now? Or – and this was what I was really afraid of – was the material a bit too old for an almost six-year-old?

We'd tried to be as faithful as possible to the book, so some of the language we were using was a little old-fashioned. There was Petrova complaining about having to change out of her 'combinations' (we had to look that up. It's some kind of old-fashioned underwear that's all in one piece instead of separate vest and knickers. Weird!) and the girls needing 'organdie frocks' for their auditions. Would Maisie's friends get it, or would it be over their heads? Was the play just too long and too serious for their age?

I didn't mention my concerns to the others. For one thing, they seemed to have troubles enough of their own.

Ruby's dancing was perfect, but she was struggling a bit with her lines. 'I just can't seem to remember what comes after "Of course I curtsied too,"' she wailed. 'I think I've got it firmly lodged in my brain, but then once I get up on the stage it's gone. It's like it's just floated out of my head and the harder I try to grab on to it the quicker it disappears.'

Then Meg had a brainwave. 'I know. Do what Posy does in the book,' she said.

'What do you mean?' Ruby asked.

'Don't you remember?' Meg said. 'Pauline wants Posy to learn their birthday vow so she can say it on her own, and Posy decides to learn it with her feet. She makes up a little dance to represent the words, and that helps her to remember.'

Ruby looked doubtful. 'I can try, I suppose. But I'm not sure my brain works that way.'

Laura was word-perfect, but she found the Russian accent difficult. Again Meg came to the rescue. She showed Laura videos of Russian accents on YouTube and said each line with her over and over again until it finally seemed to click with her.

Meg herself was doing brilliantly as Petrova. She seemed

a total natural, and even without her costume she was transformed into the stubborn, awkward, feisty Petrova as soon as she stepped onto the stage. Watching her, I realised what a good actress she was – it didn't even matter that she was fair-haired when Petrova was meant to be dark-haired – she was just so convincing in the role that that didn't matter. But off the stage, Meg was often distracted, and she still hadn't told her mum we were putting on a show.

My mum, on the other hand, was a little TOO enthusiastic, as became clear when she started casually inviting random people to come and watch the show.

'I dropped back your library books earlier,' she told me as she dished out lasagne for dinner. 'Rebecca was there, so I invited her to your show.'

'What?' I said. 'Why?'

Mum looked surprised. 'I just thought she'd like to see it. You've all been working so hard, and the little bits I've seen have been wonderful.'

'Thanks,' I murmured, taking two of the plates to bring over to the table. Mum had clearly meant it well, so I didn't want to complain, but the thought of Rebecca being at the show made me feel nervous.

Next day Mum mentioned that she'd seen Miss Doherty in Tesco, and had invited her too. Miss Doherty was Maisie's teacher, and was a lovely, warm, kind lady who adored small children. I'd had her in junior infants too and she was still my favourite teacher. I sighed to myself. At least she wouldn't be critical – she was too nice.

Then it was, 'Oh, your uncle John said he'd drop by with a birthday present for Maisie, so I told him to be sure to arrive in time for the show.' And, 'Dad told me to tell you he invited a few of the neighbours to the show before he left for China. You don't mind, do you?'

Aaaaagh! This was getting out of hand. 'Mum, no more,' I said firmly. 'This is Maisie's birthday party, don't forget! We're getting ready to entertain a bunch of five- and six-year-olds, but that's it.'

'I don't know what you're so worried about,' Mum said. 'It's only a few extra people. Once you're up on that stage you won't even know who's in the audience. Now, can you hang out that load of washing for me?'

I picked up the laundry basket and stomped off towards the garden. Didn't Mum realise how nervous I was? Then a thought struck me, and I dropped the basket on the lawn and went back into the kitchen. 'Mum, what neighbours has Dad invited?'

'Just the O'Donnells, and the Masons, and I think he might have mentioned it to the Gavins,' Mum said. 'Not the Dunnes, if that's what you're worried about. I know you and Tracey don't exactly see eye to eye.'

'Oh God, I wasn't even thinking of them,' I said. 'Tracey will probably sit at her bedroom window laughing at us like she did when we were rehearsing. I was just thinking – um – you haven't said anything to Cordelia, have you?'

'No, I haven't seen her around,' Mum said. 'I'll be sure to ask her the next time I see her.'

'Can you just leave it for a bit?' I asked.

'Why?'

'Welllll ...' I didn't look at her. 'It's just that Meg hasn't exactly told her about the show just yet.'

'Why ever not?' Mum looked puzzled.

'I'm not sure, to be honest,' I said. 'There's something a bit odd going on with them and Meg won't say much about it.'

'What do you mean, something odd?'

I was rescued by Zach and Bobby tumbling into the room demanding snacks. Mum turned to the fridge, knowing she wouldn't get a minute's peace until they were fed, and I quickly went back to the laundry, thinking that if I was lucky Mum would just let it go.

I should have known that wouldn't happen. Mum asked me about it again when she came up to my room to kiss me goodnight.

'So what's all this about Meg not telling Cordelia about your show?'

I smoothed down the edges of my duvet cover and tried to decide how to answer. 'I don't know really,' I said at last. 'Maybe it's just because they're so busy with moving to a new town and everything, maybe she thought her mum had enough to think about.' I realised as I said it how pathetic that sounded.

'But you said there was something weird going on,' Mum persisted. 'What is it?'

'Well, if I knew that, it wouldn't be weird, would it?' I said.

'I haven't been a very good neighbour, I'm afraid,' Mum sighed. 'I should have made more of an effort when they moved in – baked them a cake or something.'

I tried not to laugh. 'Mum, when's the last time you baked a cake?'

Mum pretended to be offended. 'I used to be quite the baker, I'll have you know. I just can't seem to find the time these days. Next time I see Cordelia I'll invite her over for coffee and we can have a chat. Maybe I can reassure her that you're not a bad influence on Meg, if that's what she's afraid of!'

'Good idea,' I said, relieved that the interrogation seemed to be over.

'And then we'll have to tell her about the show. It's on a Saturday afternoon, don't forget – it would be a bit strange not to tell her when it's happening right next door!'

But something was to happen before Mum got to speak to Cordelia – something that changed all our plans completely.

Chapter Fifteen

'Look at the time!' Mum exclaimed, jumping up from the breakfast table. 'I need to get dressed, Maisie's appointment is in twenty minutes. Can you keep an eye on the little ones for me?' She drained the last mouthful of tea and set her cup down beside the sink.

'Sure,' I said, looking up from my *Ballet Shoes* script. I was trying to figure out what Pauline's reaction should be in the last scene, when Posy comes home and tells them she wants to go to Czechoslovakia to train at a famous ballet school. Pauline would be excited for Posy, of course, but maybe a little bit exasperated that her little sister had gone off and made arrangements for herself without thinking of how it affected the rest of the family. Well, at least I could sympathise there, I thought.

Mum handed Emma a piece of toast. Emma immediately started licking off the jam.

'Don't want to go to the dentist,' Maisie pouted. 'It's not fair.'

'You'll be fine, Maisie,' I said. 'It's just a check-up.'

'I'll be as quick as I can,' Mum called, rushing off. 'Boys, can you tidy up the hall? There are toys everywhere, someone is going to break their neck!' This last bit was a roar as she ran up the stairs.

'I'll tell them,' I called back to her. I glanced out the back door – the boys were happily playing some sort of exploring game. It seemed a pity to haul them in just to tidy up – I'd give them a few more minutes.

Maisie was still sulking. 'I don't want the dentist to say I can't have any sweets on my birthday.'

I tried not to smile. 'She won't say that. She'll just remind you that you shouldn't have them every day, and to brush your teeth properly, and to floss and all that stuff.'

Emma had finished licking the jam off her toast and was now smearing the toast all over her highchair tray. She seemed perfectly happy, so I went back to *Ballet Shoes*. Pauline would be worried too, of course, about signing a contract with a film company when what she really wanted was to work in the theatre. I looked over Pauline's lines and tried out different inflections in my head, figuring out where her different emotions would show.

Emma was just starting to make the grumbly noises that meant, 'I'm bored of this now, take me out of my highchair please' when Bobby came crashing into the kitchen. 'Where's Mum?'

'She's getting dressed,' I told him. 'What's up?'

'Zach's stuck up the tree!' Bobby said.

'What?!' I jumped to my feet and looked out the patio doors. Sure enough, Zach was clinging on to a branch of the tree, way higher than he had ever climbed before. He looked scared half to death.

'How did he get up there?'

'He just did. I don't think he knew how high it was until he looked down,' Bobby said.

'I'm coming, Zach. You'll be OK,' I called to him, trying to sound calmer than I felt.

Emma's grumbles had turned into shouts.

'Maisie, can you watch Emma for a minute please?' I asked her. 'Play with her, but don't take her out of the highchair.'

'I have to do everything around here,' Maisie complained, but she started playing peekaboo with Emma, hiding behind a tea towel someone had thrown on the chair.

I ran out to the garden and tried to reassure Zach. 'Wow, Zach, I didn't know you were such a good climber!'

'I'm not,' Zach said. 'I'm scared. I can't get down.' His little face looked very white, peering down at me from way over my head.

'Of course you can,' I told him. 'You got up, didn't you? All you have to do is reverse it now!'

'I can't,' Zach said. 'I'm too scared.'

'Look, put your right foot onto that branch just below you, see? And then slide your hands along the branch you're on.'

'I can't,' Zach repeated, clinging firmly to the branch.

I could see I was going to have to go up and get him. I turned to Bobby. 'Will you make sure Maisie and Emma are OK? I don't want Maisie to lift Emma out of the highchair, she might drop her.'

'I'll tell her you said she's not allowed,' Bobby promised.

I started climbing the tree, glad I was wearing my runners with good grips. I got to Zach quite quickly, but I knew that talking him down was going to take a bit longer. 'OK, I've got you, Zach,' I told him. 'I'm holding on to you, so you're not going to fall. Now can you try putting your foot on the next branch?'

Zach was just reaching down to try when there was a screech from the upstairs window. Mum had spotted us. 'What's going on? Zach, are you OK?'

'He's fine, Mum,' I shouted back. 'I'm just helping him down.'

'Hang on, Zach,' Mum yelled. 'I'm coming.'

A minute later there was another screech from the kitchen – Maisie this time. What on earth was going on? Stuck up the tree, there wasn't much I could do about it, so I concentrated on Zach. Bit by bit, I persuaded him to edge slowly back along the branch, then drop to the one below.

I wondered why Mum hadn't appeared. Maybe she was sorting out whatever was wrong with Maisie. I was guessing that she had tried to take Emma out of her highchair and Bobby had tried to stop her. Probably the two of them were in a full-scale battle by now, which Emma would more than likely think was great fun.

We were almost down when Bobby came running into the garden, yelling for me once more.

'What is it?' I asked, dropping down onto the grass and reaching up to help Zach, who still seemed to be in a state of shock. 'Is Emma crying? What's wrong with Maisie?'

'It's Mum,' Bobby said. 'Come quickly.'

By now Zach was safely on the ground, looking pale but relieved. I flew into the kitchen, straight past Emma who was screaming blue murder in her highchair, and into the front hall where Maisie was shouting for me. Mum was lying at the bottom of the stairs, her face screwed up in pain. 'Oh, Hannah, I think I've broken something,' she said. 'I can't move my foot.'

Her foot was bent at an awkward angle. I rushed to her side to help her sit up. 'What happened?'

'I was running to see what was going on down here and I slipped on some toy. I told you someone was going to break their neck!' She managed a weak laugh. 'I need to get to Emma. What's wrong with her?'

'She's fine. She just wants to get out,' I said.

Zach had appeared in the hallway. 'Zach, can you lift Emma out of her highchair? Not you, Maisie, you know you're not tall enough! I want you to stay here with Mum.'

Zach raced back to the kitchen, and I followed him. I got a bag of frozen peas from the freezer and wrapped them in a tea towel. My mind was racing – what was the best thing to do? Normally I'd phone Dad in work and get him to come home – but Dad was thousands of miles away in China.

I came back out to the hall and pressed the peas to Mum's ankle. 'Look, Maisie, can you hold the peas here like this?' I showed her what to do.

'Mum, I'm going to go and see if Ruby's mum is at home,' I told her. 'You need to go to the hospital.'

Mum had turned as white as a sheet and was leaning back against Maisie, who was being really sweet and stroking her hair. She didn't object, so I grabbed the keys from the hook and ran.

I ran all the way to Ruby's house before I remembered that this was the time her mum would be dropping her to ballet camp. I knocked on the door anyway and waited a minute, but there was no answer.

Starting to feel a bit desperate, I looked all around the green. We had lots of nice neighbours we could call on, but it was the wrong time of day – some people would be in work – and the wrong time of year – a few families were gone on their holidays.

Then I thought of Meg. She and her mum should be at home.

Without thinking about it any more, I ran to Meg's house and banged on the door.

Cordelia was amazing. As soon as I told her what had happened, she just grabbed her phone and keys and dashed over to our house, hopping over the wall as easily as Meg. She was the voice of absolute calm, telling Mum that everything was going to be OK and reassuring Bobby, who was distraught about not tidying up the cars, that accidents just happen and it wasn't his fault.

I was so relieved to have a grown-up in charge that I felt like crying, though I managed to hold back the tears. If I cried now the others would go to pieces completely.

'Now Claire, we're going to need to get this silly old ankle looked at,' Cordelia said. 'Hannah and I will help you out to the car, and we'll be off to the hospital before you can say Jiminy Cricket. Last time I was at the hospital there was the most terribly handsome young doctor on duty. I do hope he's working today. Almost worth getting injured for, darling. Now Hannah, you come this side of your mum and help me to support her out to the car.'

Mum was still deathly pale and didn't protest as Cordelia and I helped her up. Zach cleared a path through the toys and Bobby opened the door wide so the three of us could fit through. Mum kept her injured foot raised and managed to hop along, leaning heavily on Cordelia and me and wincing with the pain.

Meg opened the car door and we helped Mum in.

'Hannah ...' she started to say.

'Don't worry Mum, everything will be fine,' I said firmly. 'I'll look after everyone while Cordelia takes you to the hospital. You'll be home before you know it!'

'I'll help her,' Meg told Mum, putting her arm around me.

Mum smiled wanly as Cordelia closed the door and made her way around to the driver's side.

'Take care, darlings – I'll phone the moment we know anything,' she said.

The car sped off. I couldn't hold the tears back any longer. Meg held me tight for a minute as I just sobbed. Then I wiped my tears away and turned to my siblings, who were looking at me in shock (except Emma, who was trying to eat Bobby's shoelace).

'Sorry, guys. Mum will be fine. I just got a fright,' I

told them.

I led the way inside, picking Emma up and removing the shoelace from her mouth.

'At least I don't have to go to the dentist,' Maisie said.

Chapter Sixteen

Mum's ankle was broken.

Cordelia called to tell me the news, saying she knew I'd be anxious to hear. 'The doctor has given her something for the pain, so she's pretty wiped out,' she told me. 'I'm going to bring her home now and I think the poor lamb had better just go to bed for the afternoon.'

'Oh poor Mum,' I said. 'Is she going to be on crutches for a few weeks?'

'Yes.' Cordelia hesitated. 'She'll be able to get about on crutches a bit, but Hannah darling, the doctor is simply insisting that she stay off her feet as much as possible for the next fortnight.'

My heart sank. Mum – laid up for a fortnight? How would she cope with not being able to get around? And how would the rest of us cope without her?

'When is your dad due back from China?' Cordelia asked.

'Not for another week,' I told her. I tried to sound as cheerful as I could. 'It's OK, we'll be fine.'

'Now you're not to worry about a thing,' Cordelia said. 'I'll help as much as I can. I'm in work this week so I won't be around much, but I can get some shopping in for you, and I'll make you a pasta bake tomorrow. Heaven knows I'm not much of a cook, but I can manage a pasta bake all right!'

'Thanks, that's so nice of you,' I said.

The enormity of what this would mean was just starting to hit me. Looking after four children (even though I knew Zach, at least, would be a help), making sure we were all fed, taking care of Mum in her sick bed, and trying to keep Emma from poisoning herself (I had to put down the phone for a minute to take a chunk of modelling clay away from her). My head was whirling trying to plan ahead as best I could. I wished Mum was home so I could see for myself how she was. And I wished I could talk to Dad and tell him what had happened, but I thought I'd better wait until Mum was home.

Half an hour later Cordelia's car pulled up outside the house. I ran out and opened the passenger door. Mum looked even paler than she had earlier, but she smiled at me and said 'Don't worry Hannah, I'm going to be fine.'

With my support she struggled to her feet. 'I've got crutches, but I think I'm going to need a bit of practice getting used to them,' she told me.

'Just leave the crutches for now, you can lean on me,' I said.

Cordelia came around to take the other side and we slowly made our way into the sitting room where Mum collapsed onto the couch. 'Oh, it's good to be home!'

Meg was hovering anxiously in the background. 'Can I get you anything, Claire? Do you want a cup of tea?'

'No, I'm fine thanks. I think I'll just have a little sleep,' Mum said, stretching out. She looked half asleep already.

I took the cosy purple throw and spread it carefully over her. 'Yes, just have a sleep Mum, you'll feel better.'

Zach and Maisie were peering around the door. I shooed them out. 'Mum needs some rest, you can see her later, OK?'

Cordelia was getting ready to leave. 'Meg and I need to call over to see her grandparents now Hannah, but I'll check in later to see how you are.'

'We'll be fine,' I said, trying to sound confident. 'Thanks so much for all your help.'

'Oh, don't mention it,' Cordelia said. 'Your mum would do just the same for me! I'm just sorry we didn't get to see that handsome doctor. Such a disappointment. Take it easy this afternoon – a nice quiet activity maybe!'

'We will,' I said.

Meg gave me a hug. 'Good luck, Hannah! I'll see you later.'

Once I had waved them off I took Mum's phone and sent Dad a text, asking him to Skype me. I took out the iPad and immediately got involved in an argument with Bobby, who wanted to play games on it.

'But why can't I use it?' he whined.

'Because I need it, OK?' I told him.

'Can I have it after you?'

'I'll see.'

'Mum said we're allowed to use it on weekends once we've tidied our rooms!'

'Oh, have you tidied your room?' I asked, knowing he hadn't.

'I'll do it now, then it's my turn, OK?'

I was saved by Dad's photo flashing up on the screen. I pressed answer. 'Hi, Dad!'

'Hi, Hannah! Hi, Maisie!'

Maisie had appeared behind me.

'I'm having the best time,' Dad told us. 'We had no meetings today so our hosts took us to see the Great Wall of China. What a sight! You wouldn't believe it, girls. So what's going on with you?'

'Mum broke her ankle,' Maisie said.

'Maisie!' I'd been planning to break the news a bit more gently.

'What?!' Dad looked aghast.

'She was screaming and screaming and an ambulance had to come and go nee-naw nee-naw and speed her off to hospital so they could save her life,' Maisie went on.

'Seriously?'

'Maisie, stop exaggerating!' I told her. I turned to Dad. 'It wasn't like that, Dad. Mum is OK. And we didn't need an ambulance – Cordelia took her to the hospital. But she did break her ankle. She fell down the stairs.'

'Oh no. Where is she now?' Dad demanded.

'She's asleep on the couch,' I told him. I explained to him, a bit less dramatically than Maisie, exactly what had happened. Dad looked very upset, and I could see he was trying to work out how to handle this. Suddenly I found myself wishing harder than ever that he was here to give me a hug and tell me everything was going to be OK.

'Don't worry, girls. I'm sure Mum will be fine,' Dad said. 'Maisie, have you been doing any drawings this week? Can you find some and show me?'

'Does that mean you want to talk to Hannah on your own?' Maisie asked. That girl really doesn't miss much.

Dad laughed. 'I do actually. Can you give us a few minutes?'

'Yes. You only had to ask,' Maisie informed him. 'I need to get back to my game anyway.'

Dad waited until she'd moved away. 'I should have known Maisie would see right through me,' he said with a grin. 'Hannah, I don't want you to disturb Mum now, but get her to Skype me as soon as she wakes up, OK?'

'Won't it be the middle of the night there?' I asked him. We'd talked on Skype a few times that week and it was always mid-afternoon for us while Dad was just about to go to bed. The kitchen clock said it was nearly 4pm, so I knew it must be pretty late in China.

'That doesn't matter,' Dad said. 'I'll leave my phone on the bed beside me. I'm going to check out flights now, see if I can come home earlier.'

'No, you don't need to do that, Dad,' I said. 'We'll be fine – it's only another six days.'

'But how will you manage? The boys are a handful, never mind feeding Emma, and changing her, and looking after Maisie too. And what about meals?'

'Meg's mum said she'd help out,' I told him. 'And I'm sure Ruby's mum will too, once she finds out. Really, we'll be OK.'

Dad was scratching his beard, which always means he's thinking. After a minute, he said, 'Well, I'll talk to Mum later and see what she thinks. But if you can manage I really would like to stay for the next two meetings at least. It's so important for the business, you see.'

'I know. It'll be fine, really,' I said.

Bobby came running back into the room. 'Hannah, I've finished tidying, can I have the iPad now? Oh, hi, Dad!'

'Hi, Bobby. What's this I hear, tidying your room? What's come over you?'

'He wants to play games on the iPad,' I said, laughing. 'He's allowed once his room is tidy.'

'Well, I'd better let you go so,' Dad said. 'Where's Zach?'

'He's walking Emma around the garden in her pram,' I told him. 'She wouldn't fall asleep so he said he'd try that.'

Dad smiled. 'I'd forgotten what a great help Zach can be. Maybe you will be OK after all.'

'Of course we will,' I said.

'We can Skype again tomorrow, so tell Zach I said hello and I'll talk to him then. And tell Maisie I'll see her pictures then too. Bye, kids!'

Dad's image disappeared from the screen.

'Can I have it now, Hannah?' Bobby asked.

I handed him the iPad – at least that would keep him busy for a few minutes. Zach was still patiently walking Emma up and down the garden, and Maisie hadn't reappeared. I realised I'd better start thinking about dinner. I knew Mum wouldn't mind if I ordered a pizza delivery, but I was determined not to go for the easy option. I wanted to show Dad that I could cope with things here, so he wouldn't feel he had to rush home. I knew how important this trip was to him. I reached for Mum's cookbook. I'd seen her make curry thousands of times – how hard could it be?

An hour later I was beginning to regret ever having heard of curry. The first lot of rice had got burnt and stuck to the bottom of the saucepan. The second lot was taking forever to cook because I was afraid to turn the heat up too high. The curry looked a completely different colour from when Mum made it, and was starting to get all congealed looking because it had been ready for ages while I was busy burning the rice. The sink was piled high with dirty dishes and the countertops were covered with vegetable peelings and empty tins which I hadn't had a chance to clear away yet.

'Hannah, I'm starving. Is dinner nearly ready?' asked Bobby.

'Nearly.' I looked anxiously at the rice.

Zach peered over my shoulder. 'We could have naan bread instead of rice,' he suggested.

'Good idea,' I told him. 'Why don't you get some out?'

Zach started rummaging in the cupboard, while I switched off the hob and started stirring the curry again. It definitely didn't look right, but it probably wouldn't kill us.

'I don't think we have any.' Zach's voice was muffled from the depths of the cupboard.

'Let me look.' I moved him out of the way, but he was right – no naan bread.

'But I'm HUNGRY!' Bobby whined.

'We'll just have to have toast with it,' I said. 'Stop whining, Bobby. If you set the table we'll be ready to eat quicker.'

I started making toast, kind of glad Mum was still asleep and couldn't see what a mess I'd made of dinner. Pizza was definitely the way to go tomorrow, I decided.

It was a really weird dinner. Maisie absolutely refused to eat the curry because 'it's not meant to be that colour', so I made her a banana sandwich instead. Zach ate some and tried to convince Bobby it tasted fine, but Bobby just ate the toast. I was so fed up of the smell of cooking that I wasn't even hungry any more. I took the big pot of leftover curry and silently scraped it into the bin.

Mum woke up in time to feed Emma. I decided to skip her bath for once and managed to get her to bed, although I was interrupted about seventeen times by Maisie who couldn't find the pyjamas she wanted and didn't like any of my alternative suggestions. Then she couldn't find Flopsy, her blue bunny who she can't sleep without. Then she wanted me to read her a story, and wouldn't let Zach when he offered to read it instead.

Finally they were all in bed. I came downstairs, saw the mountain of dishes waiting for me in the kitchen and walked straight back out again. They'd just have to wait – I'd had enough, I collapsed on the couch beside Mum, too tired even to flick channels. I thought about all I'd had to do that afternoon, and how I hadn't even done half the things properly, and how there were still another six days of this to go.

Something was going to have to give. And that something would be Star Club.

Chapter Seventeen

I rang the girls the next morning to arrange an emergency meeting of Star Club for that afternoon. Ruby offered to have it at her house.

I was dreading breaking the news to my friends that we'd have to cancel the show. I could just picture their faces – after all the hard work we'd put in, it was heartbreaking not to be able to go through with our performance. And whenever I thought about my own part, I got a lump in my throat. I'd put my heart and soul into transforming myself into Pauline these last few weeks. The thought that I'd never get to bring her to life in front of an audience was too much to bear.

It was pouring rain as I walked over to Ruby's house. The weather seemed to match my mood.

'Thanks for coming, everyone,' I said when we had all taken up our usual spots in Ruby's bedroom. 'I'm afraid I've got some bad news.'

I explained what had happened to Mum, and how she was going to be laid up for the rest of the week, and how

Dad wasn't due back from China until Friday, the day before Maisie's party.

'I'm sorry, guys,' I said at last. 'But you know what this means, don't you? We're going to have to call off the show.'

'What?' cried Ruby. 'Call it off completely?'

'I'm afraid so,' I said. 'I'm going to have to be at home all the time so I can help Mum with the kids and everything. I'm just not going to have time to rehearse any more. I was only able to get away now because I put on a DVD for them.'

'But what about Maisie's party?' Laura asked. 'That's still going ahead, isn't it?'

'The party will,' I said. 'We can't cancel it, she'd be devastated. Dad and I will just have to organise some games for her friends – Pass the Parcel and Musical Chairs and all that sort of thing. But we can't do the show. And at least it means I can cancel all those extra people Mum invited to it.' I managed a shaky laugh.

Ruby looked distraught. Laura was trying to be understanding, but she was clearly upset too. Only Meg looked as calm as ever.

'You know,' Meg said suddenly, 'we're a drama club. We're only twelve years old, but we've worked really hard to make it the best drama club we can. And there's a saying in show business that I think we need to remember. The show must go on.'

'What do you mean?' I asked.

'The show must go on,' Meg repeated. 'It means no matter what happens, if the leading lady is sick, if the costumes aren't delivered on time, if you've forgotten your lines, it doesn't matter. You have an audience who have come to see you perform, and you'd better make sure you give them what they've come to see.'

'Meg's right,' Laura said suddenly. 'We're Star Club. We can't just give up at the first sign of trouble. The show must go on!'

I sighed. 'But how can it? We're just not ready yet, and I'm not going to be able to help you guys organise any of the things that need to be done.'

'We can split up the jobs between us,' Laura said. 'It's only getting the last few props and doing up some programmes. We'll manage.'

'But what about rehearsals?' I said. 'You can't manage without Pauline. And I'm just not going to have time. The only way would be if I brought the whole gang with me.'

'Then do it,' Meg said calmly.

'OK, Meg, I don't think you know Hannah's little brothers well enough yet, or you wouldn't be saying that,' Laura laughed. 'If you're expecting them to sit quietly and watch us rehearse you're going to be pretty disappointed.'

'I'm not.' Meg still sounded remarkably calm. 'No one wants to sit quietly and watch everyone else perform.

Zach and Bobby can be in it. Maisie too.'

I stared at her incredulously. 'Meg, have you gone completely crazy? I mean, I know Maisie would love to be in the show, but the only way Zach and Bobby would do it is if they can give a demonstration of fighting with lightsabers in a galaxy far far away.'

'Well then, that's what they'll have to do,' Meg said, shrugging her shoulders.

I looked at the others. Laura had tilted her head to one side and was considering carefully. Ruby's eyes had widened to their fullest extent. 'But – but – but ...' she stammered. 'I mean, it's *Ballet Shoes*!'

'Not any more.' Meg was firm. 'It's a variety show.'

'What's a variety show?' Ruby asked.

'It's like it says. It's a mixture of different acts. We pick a few scenes from *Ballet Shoes*, the ones we think we can do best without too many rehearsals. We put in a *Star Wars* scene for the boys. And then something for Maisie. Basically mix it all up.'

I suddenly felt a tiny bit excited again. 'Can we really do it in such a short time?' I asked.

'Of course we can,' Laura said. 'We'll keep it as simple as we can.'

'You know, I think this just might work,' I said, breaking into a smile. 'Actually, Maisie's friends might like it even better. To be honest, I was starting to wonder if our *Ballet*

Shoes show was going to be too hard for them to follow.'

'I was a bit worried about that too,' Laura admitted. 'We didn't really have six-year-olds in mind when we started planning it.'

'Well, maybe the first thing we should do is appoint Maisie as a junior consultant,' Meg said. 'We can try things out on her and ask her opinion on what will work.'

'She will LOVE that,' I said.

I glanced over at Ruby. She still hadn't said very much. I knew she was bound to be feeling upset that we weren't going to be focusing solely on her beloved *Ballet Shoes*. 'What do you think, Ruby?' I asked.

'I think it will be great,' Ruby said, putting on a determined smile. 'It's not exactly what I had in mind, but things change. I think we can put on a really good show.'

'And your ballet will still be a really important part of it,' I told her.

'Actually, since it's a variety show now, why not have a ballet solo from Ruby on its own – separate from the *Ballet Shoes* scene?' Meg suggested. 'You could do the dance you're working on for your exam.'

Ruby's face brightened at once. 'Could I really? I've been working so hard on it – it would be nice to get a bit of encouragement.'

'Of course,' I said. 'It'd be perfect.'

'We're definitely putting the variety into variety show,'

Laura giggled.

I looked around at my friends. 'You guys are amazing,' I said. 'I really thought we'd have to abandon our show, but now I think it's going to be better than ever!'

The rain had cleared up and the sun was just trying to come out as we left Ruby's. Meg and I walked home together, chatting about which scenes were almost perfect and which would be OK with a bit more work. I had a warm glow inside knowing I was going to be able to play Pauline after all. I planned to grab every spare minute that I could to practise.

I still had one barrier to overcome when I got home. Well, two, to be precise. I knew Maisie would be absolutely thrilled to be involved in the show. But Zach and Bobby were another story.

It was time for some big-sister mind games.

Chapter Eighteen

I was a little bit worried that Maisie would decide to be contrary and say she didn't want to be in the show any more now that I wanted her to be. But she was too excited at the idea to make things difficult.

'Can I do singing? And dancing? And acting?' she wanted to know. 'Can I be a dog? Or a cat?'

'Maybe just one of those things,' I said cautiously. 'We've got a lot of acts to fit in, and we don't want to run out of time. Which one do you want to do the most?'

'I don't know,' Maisie said. 'I'll need to think about it. Probably singing. No, dancing. Actually, maybe acting. I definitely want to be a dog, anyway.'

'You could sing that song you were learning in school,' I suggested.

'Raindrops on roses?' asked Maisie. That was her name for 'My Favourite Things' from *The Sound of Music*.

'That's the one.'

'Maybe.' Maisie didn't sound convinced. 'I'd rather do something *new* though.'

'You could do your own version of it,' I said. 'You know, put in some actions or something, or maybe even change the words.'

'That's a good idea!' Maisie exclaimed. 'Thanks, Hannah. My own favourite things …'

I wondered what she would come up with. At least it would be easier than starting from scratch to try to teach her something new. There really wasn't enough time.

'I'm going to go and practise now,' she announced, scrambling down from the table.

'OK, but can you not tell the boys what you're doing?' I asked her. 'I want to talk to them about it myself.'

'Are THEY going to be in the show?' Maisie didn't look too impressed at the idea.

'We'll see,' I said.

The boys were in the garden playing *Star Wars* yet again. It seemed like a good opportunity to bring up the subject.

'Wow, you two really look the part,' I said. 'It's so cool to watch you. I feel like I'm on another planet or something.'

Zach looked at me suspiciously. 'I thought you hated *Star Wars*.'

Oops. Maybe I'd laid it on a bit too thick.

'No, of course not!' I said. 'I mean, maybe I don't like you being too noisy when I'm trying to talk to my friends or something, but it's great to watch you! Can you show me what you were doing?'

Bobby immediately launched himself at Zach, who, caught off guard, ended up sprawling on the lawn.

'Ha! Got you!' Bobby said.

'That's not fair, I wasn't ready!' Zach protested. 'Hannah, tell him!'

'Why don't you start again?' I said, helping Zach to his feet. 'When I count to three, OK?'

I counted to three, and this time both boys charged at each other with their lightsabers. I watched them battle it out for about five minutes, chasing each other around the garden and even jumping on top of the garden table to continue the fight there.

'Brilliant!' I said. 'Really, you're so convincing. I bet you'd love to be able to show people how much you can do.'

'What do you mean?' Zach asked.

I decided it was time to come clean. 'Here's the thing. How would you like to be in the show I'm doing with my friends?'

'That ballet thing?' Bobby looked disgusted.

I rushed to explain. 'It's not just ballet any more. We're making it into a variety show. We're going to have lots of different things in it, and you could do a *Star Wars* scene if you like.'

'Yeah! Can I do this?' Bobby showed me an overhead kick that looked like it was designed to knock my teeth out. I ducked just in time.

'Yes, just not in my face!' I told him. 'Be careful!' I looked at Zach. 'What do you think, Zach?'

'I'm not sure,' Zach said. He was looking down at the ground.

'Oh pleeeeeease!' said Bobby. 'I can't do it on my own.'

Zach had always been a lot shyer than Bobby. I knew he would be feeling nervous about people watching him.

'We could keep it pretty short,' I said. 'Just the moves you feel you know really well, maybe? And you have all week to practise – I'm sure you'll be able to give a great demonstration!'

'Maybe,' Zach said.

'I can help you with it too, watch you practising and all that,' I said.

'Oh pleeeeease!' Bobby said again.

Zach still wasn't giving in.

'Oh well.' I got up from my seat on the edge of the patio. 'Maybe Maisie will do it with you, Bobby. I could give you another job to do, Zach. Like cleaning up or something? Because everyone has to help out at the party, it's going to be a really busy day. Maybe you could be in charge of picking up all the cups and things that get left lying around? You know what Maisie's friends are like.'

'No! I'm not cleaning up!' Zach said. 'I'll be in the show, OK? Just as long as we keep it short.'

I smiled. 'No problem.'

Maisie came running out to the garden. 'Hannah, Mum wants you to take Emma.'

I sighed. No chance of a bit of time to myself then.

Mum was sitting on the floor building a tower block for Emma, but Emma seemed to have lost all interest in knocking it over and was just whining.

'Oh, Hannah, there you are, I'm glad you're back,' Mum said. 'I've run out of things I can do with Emma sitting on the floor. I never thought she'd get bored of having my undivided attention, but looks like it's finally happened!'

'I'll take her out to the garden,' I said. 'Do you need anything first? Cup of tea?'

'A cup of tea would be wonderful,' Mum said, leaning back against the couch. 'Thank you, honey. It's so frustrating not being able to do anything for myself – or for you lot.'

I felt bad for complaining. I knew Mum had it so much worse than me. 'Don't worry, it's no problem. We're managing fine.'

'But you're having to do so much – it's not fair. It's taking over your summer holidays. What about Star Club?'

'Actually, Meg came up with a great idea.'

'Did she? Oh, that reminds me, I didn't get a chance to talk to Cordelia yesterday. Everything was so crazy. But she's so nice – she was wonderful, wasn't she? I'm sure everything will be fine if Meg tells her about the show. What was the idea, anyway?'

I told her all about how Maisie's birthday entertainment was now going to be a variety show, complete with acting, dancing, singing and of course *Star Wars*.

'I'm being a dog,' Maisie informed Mum, crawling into the room and pretending to bite Emma, which made her laugh. 'A dog that sings about its favourite things.'

I rolled my eyes at Mum. It sounded like Maisie's act was going to need a bit of work.

Chapter Nineteen

'Hannah, can you tell Bobby to stop lunging at me like that? He's ruining my kicks!'

'Hannah, have you seen my costume?'

'Hannah, which do you think sounds better – "Raindrops on bones and chasing kittens", or "raindrops on kennels and scaring kittens"?'

'Hannah, Mum says can you take Emma?'

Ever get sick of the sound of your own name?

I'd been practising with the kids all week, and now I was trying to get them organised for the dress rehearsal. It was the first time we'd be running through the whole show in the order we'd be performing it in. The rest of Star Club would be arriving any minute, and we were still running around like headless chickens.

Maisie was singing first one version of the line and then the other, over and over again, and slightly out of tune.

'Your costume is on Mum's bed,' I told Bobby. 'They're all up there – I told you that already. And stop lunging at Zach. Maisie, please stop singing!'

'I'm just trying to work out which one is better!' Maisie told me in a hurt voice. 'You said I should practise!'

'I know. We'll all practise together in a minute, OK?'

'HANNAH!' This time it was Mum.

'She wants you to take Emma,' Zach reminded me.

'I know! I can't do everything at once! We'll have to bring her out to the garden with us, but I don't know what I'm going to do with her while we're rehearsing.'

'We could put her in the travel cot,' Zach suggested. 'She likes that – for about five minutes anyway.'

'Good idea,' I said. 'Can you and Bobby bring it out-side?'

'HANNAH!'

'Coming, Mum!'

I rushed into the sitting room to find Mum attempting to struggle to her feet. 'Oh, don't get up, Mum!' I said. 'What do you need?'

'Look at Emma!' she told me.

I turned around. Emma was standing up holding on to the TV unit, a big grin on her chubby little face.

'Oh wow, Emma! You're standing!'

It was the first time Emma had stood up on her own, and she looked delighted with herself.

'She sure knows how to pick her moments,' Mum said with a laugh. 'None of the rest of you were standing up until you were ten months at least. We're going to need another whole level of babyproofing!'

I looked around the room. Mum and Dad had baby-proofed everything that Emma could reach by crawling around the room. The DVDs had all been moved to higher shelves (after Emma had wrecked a couple of the cardboard covers by chewing on the corners) and Dad had put a protective sponge cover on the edges of the hearth so Emma wouldn't bang her head. But now that she was standing she could reach the ornaments on the bookshelves, the candles on the little table and the plant on the TV unit. Which she was currently trying to eat.

'Emma!' I exclaimed. 'That's not for eating!' I picked her up and she immediately started to howl. 'I know, I'm so cruel not letting you eat an orchid,' I told her.

I turned to Mum. 'I can take her out to the garden for a while if you like.'

'But what about your rehearsal?' Mum asked.

'I'll put her in the travel cot, and we can take it in turns to mind her if she gets fed up of that,' I said.

'Well, if you don't mind, I could do with a rest,' Mum admitted. 'My ankle is really hurting, and the painkillers are making me feel sleepy.'

'We'll be fine,' I said. 'I can bring her back in if it gets too much.'

'Please do.' Mum was already leaning her head back against the couch, her eyes closed.

I glanced out the window and saw Ruby coming up the drive. Laura was just behind her on her bike. I went to let them in, balancing Emma on my hip.

'Hello, Emma! Are you going to be in the show too?' Ruby asked, stroking Emma's cheek.

Emma laughed.

'Don't even joke about it!' I said. 'She'd love the attention! She'll have to come to the rehearsal, though. Mum needs a rest.'

'We'll help mind her,' Ruby promised.

'I've brought the paper for the programmes,' Laura said. 'I thought we could make them after the rehearsal.'

'Oh, the programmes! I'd forgotten all about those!' I said. 'Are we going to have enough time?'

'I thought we could rope in some child labour to help out,' Laura said with a grin. 'Maisie loves art, doesn't she?'

'Great idea,' I said. 'Might even get the boys involved too, keep them out of Mum's way a bit longer.'

'Hannah!' It was Zach shouting from the garden.

'Oh my God!' I said through gritted teeth.

Ruby looked at me in surprise.

'Sorry,' I said. 'I'm just so sick of people shouting for me all the time! It hasn't stopped all morning!'

Laura was understanding. 'Come on, I'll sort Zach out. And we'll get the rehearsal set up, and you can put on your director's visor and shout at us instead!'

I couldn't help laughing. 'Thanks, you guys. I'm so lucky to have such great friends.'

Meg was already in the garden, having squeezed through the hedge as usual. She was busy setting up some of the garden chairs in a row in front of the patio. Ruby's parents had lent us all of theirs, and a few of the other neighbours had promised some too.

'Hi, guys! I thought we could sit here when we're not performing and be a proper audience.'

'Oh my goodness, it's starting to look like a real show,' Ruby said, clutching her hair dramatically.

'Well, it should, it's the dress rehearsal,' Laura pointed out. 'We've got to have everything perfect now.'

It was a long way from perfect.

Maisie kept changing the words of her song. Zach was trying to put a somersault into his routine, but he couldn't quite pull it off. Then he started complaining that Bobby wasn't sticking to the right moves. Ruby still didn't have some of her lines right, and Laura forgot to change costumes and came out wearing Madame Fidolia's shawl when she was meant to be Nana.

I sat in my director's chair and put my head in my hands. 'Are we really going on stage tomorrow?' I moaned. 'Like, in front of people?'

'Don't worry, Hannah – you know what they say – a bad dress rehearsal means a good first performance!' Meg said soothingly.

'Well then this should be the best first performance in the history of the earth!' I said.

'We've only got one performance. We have to get it right first time!' Ruby pointed out.

'Oh that's really helpful,' I snapped.

'No need to be so grouchy!' Ruby said. 'We're all nervous.'

'Sorry,' I muttered, but I wasn't really. I felt like no one else could possibly understand how I felt. They only had to worry about their own parts, but I had to pull the whole show together.

'What's going on here?' boomed a deep voice. I turned around.

'Dad!' I'd never been so glad to see him in my life. Maisie, Bobby and Zach all started screaming in delight and running towards him, but I got there first and was enveloped in one of his big bear hugs.

'Oh Dad, I'm so glad you're home,' I told him. 'We weren't expecting you until tomorrow.'

'I managed to get an earlier flight,' Dad said. 'I thought you might need some help getting ready for this fantastic show I've been hearing about.'

'We need all the help we can get,' I told him, moving aside to let the boys and Maisie have their turn.

'Oh Hannah, it's not as bad as all that,' Laura said reassuringly. 'We're getting there. Maybe we just need to take a little break.'

'Good idea,' Dad said. 'I propose ice creams all round.'

It was amazing how much better everything seemed after a break for ice cream. Feeling refreshed, we started the dress rehearsal all over again. This time it went much more smoothly. Laura remembered to change her clothes between scenes, Ruby remembered her lines, and Zach and Bobby managed to keep the fighting on a pretend level. Maisie's song was still pretty weird, but Dad whispered to me that her friends would probably love it, which was true.

'Well done, everyone,' I said at last, remembering that as director I was supposed to be encouraging them and not just criticising. 'That was great. I think it's going to be a really fantastic show!'

As we tidied up Meg took me aside and said quietly, 'Hannah, can you do me a favour? Can you come over later and help me tell Mum about the show?'

'You still haven't told her?' I exclaimed.

'I kind of kept putting it off,' Meg said. 'But I'm going to have to tell her now or she'll find out tomorrow! She should be home from work about 5.30 – can you come over then?'

'OK,' I agreed. I really hoped Cordelia wasn't going to make a fuss. The show couldn't go ahead without Meg!

Cordelia had kindly brought us over a pasta bake the day before. I used the excuse of returning the dish to pop over. Cordelia arrived just minutes after me, looking flustered.

'Thank goodness it's Friday! That computer program is simply ghastly – I'm going to have to swot up on it all over again over the weekend! What a bore!' She threw her handbag into the corner and went to switch on the coffee machine.

I wondered if it was the best time to bring up the show, but Meg plunged right in. 'Mum, I've got something to tell you.'

'Oh?' Cordelia had her back to us, taking a mug out of the cupboard.

'Hannah and Laura and Ruby and I and Hannah's brothers and sister have been practising for a show and we're going to put it on tomorrow in Hannah's garden.' Meg spoke the words quickly, as if determined to get it over and done with.

Cordelia closed the cupboard door with a bang. I was relieved to see that she looked more surprised than cross. 'Good heavens. How long has this been going on, may I ask?'

'A few weeks,' Meg said. 'I'd have told you, but I didn't want you getting upset.'

'Getting upset?' Cordelia's eyebrows were sky-high. 'I'm

not upset, darling, but you know what we agreed when we moved here.'

'I didn't agree!' Meg said. 'Anyway, this is just a small little family show, isn't it Hannah?' Meg's eyes were begging me to back her up.

'That's right,' I said. 'It's for my sister Maisie's birthday party, and it's just Maisie's friends and a few of the neighbours who are going to be coming to see it. We'd love you to come too, of course.'

'Good heavens,' Cordelia said again. 'Well, of course I'll come, darlings. I do wish you'd told me, Meg.'

'Sorry, Mum,' Meg said. 'I know I should have told you.'

Cordelia sighed. 'You really can't keep away from it all, can you? You're just like your father!'

'You're one to talk,' Meg said, but she was grinning.

I looked from one to the other, not quite sure what was going on.

Cordelia suddenly remembered I was there. 'I suppose you're the witness for the defence, Hannah, in case I went ballistic!'

'Uh … I just wanted to return your dish,' I said.

Cordelia laughed. 'I'm only teasing, darling. Now, hadn't you better run along home? Your mum will be looking for you.'

'Dad got back today, so things aren't quite so crazy,' I told her. 'But I'd better go, I'll see you tomorrow Meg.

Thanks for saying you'll come to the show, Cordelia.'

'I wouldn't miss it,' Cordelia assured me.

Chapter Twenty

After dinner (which in celebration of Dad's early return was pizza again) Dad and I started to set things up for Maisie's party. I was just helping him hang up Mum's original birthday banner (Maisie's one was going to take pride of place in the garden) when the phone rang.

'Hannah, you won't believe it.' It was Laura, sounding breathless with excitement. 'I've just seen a strange car pulling up outside Meg's granny's house, and there's a man in it talking on the phone.'

Laura has a tendency to overreact.

'It's probably someone trying to sell her a house alarm,' I said.

'What if it's Meg's dad?' Laura said. 'He looks about the right age, and he looks American.'

'How exactly does someone look American?' I asked her.

'I don't know ... sort of healthy-looking and tanned. He's got dark hair.'

I remembered the photo I'd seen on Sadie's phone. 'I

think Meg's dad has dark hair.'

'There you go then!' Laura exclaimed, as if this proved everything. 'Oh! He's getting out of the car. He's ringing the doorbell. He's talking to Meg's granny.'

I waited.

'He's going inside now! Why is she letting him in?'

'Maybe she wants to buy a house alarm,' I suggested.

'Hannah, I don't think you're taking this seriously enough! What should I do?'

'I don't know.' I was a bit more concerned about Maisie's party decorations than the fact that Laura had seen a dark-haired man who might have been Meg's father or might in fact just have been a house alarm salesman. 'Just keep an eye on things, I guess. Sorry Laura, I have to go.'

'OK, but watch out in case he heads over to Meg's house next!' Laura said. 'It's a silver car.'

I promised that I would keep an eye out. I put down the phone and went back to helping Dad.

Not long afterwards the phone rang again – this time it was Ruby. 'Are you watching Meg's house?' she wanted to know.

'I'm a bit busy here,' I told her. 'Don't tell me Laura has you spying on Meg too.'

'We're not spying.' Ruby sounded hurt. 'We're just looking out for our friend. Anyway, guess what just happened?'

'What?'

'I saw Meg and her mum come running out of the house and get into the car and drive off really quickly.'

'Is that all?'

'What do you mean, is that all? They were running! Why would they be running?'

'Maybe they needed something before the shops closed.'

Ruby sighed dramatically into the phone. 'You're no good. I'm going to ring Laura.'

I hung up. Despite what I'd said to the girls, I did find myself wondering if it could be Meg's dad who'd turned up at Sadie's house. Maybe Meg and Cordelia had rushed over to see him? Or – if Laura's kidnap theory was right – maybe they'd decided to run away?

I shook my head. I was starting to sound as crazy as Laura now. Nevertheless, I found myself going to the front window every now and again that evening, checking to see if Cordelia's car had come back. But there was still no sign of it by the time I went to bed. I started feeling a teeny tiny bit worried.

When I woke the next morning the first thing I did was rush to the window. There was Cordelia's car, parked in front of their house as usual. I heaved a sigh of relief. I still felt like I wanted to rush over to make sure Meg was all right, but I told myself that was crazy. I'd be seeing her in a few hours anyway, when she came over to get ready for the show.

Oh my God! The show! My stomach did a somersault. We were going on stage in just a couple of hours!

'Raindrops on bones and scaring kittens ...' The words were slightly muffled – Maisie's head was still under her duvet, where she often ends up at night, upside down in her bed. A head emerged from the wrong end of her bed. 'Morning, Hannah! It's my birthday – YAY!'

'Happy birthday, Maisie,' I said, giving her a kiss. 'I hope you have a fantastic day!'

'Let's go downstairs and find my presents!' Maisie said.

'Let me go first and see if Mum is awake,' I told her.

The stairs were too difficult for Mum so she had been sleeping on the couch. Emma slept beside her in her pram, so Mum could reach her easily if she needed feeding during the night. I slipped quietly downstairs, but I needn't have worried – Mum was wide awake, and Dad was up too, and already busy changing Emma's nappy.

'I couldn't sleep properly,' he told me. 'Must be the jetlag. No doubt the tiredness will hit me later!'

'As long as you can keep going until after Maisie's party,' Mum said with a laugh. 'Where's my little birthday girl?'

'I'll get her,' I said. I went out to the hall and called her. 'Maisie, you can come down!'

Maisie came tumbling down the stairs, closely followed

by Zach and Bobby. After a flurry of present-opening and singing happy birthday, Dad made a huge stack of his speciality birthday pancakes – lovely big thick ones stuffed with blueberries. I looked around the table at my family, all together again, and felt a warm glow that wasn't just being full of pancakes.

'Look at the time!' Mum exclaimed. 'We'd better get dressed. Your friends will be here in half an hour to get ready for the show, Hannah.'

My stomach did that crazy flip-flop thing again. 'Are you feeling nervous, Maisie?' I asked her, wondering if it was just me.

'About what?'

'About the show.'

Maisie opened her eyes wide. 'No. Why would I feel nervous? I'm going to be the most fantastic singing dog ever.'

I laughed, wishing I had some of her confidence. 'Of course you are. OK, let's go get into our costumes!'

Fifteen minutes later we were back downstairs, me dressed in Pauline's kilt and brown jumper and Maisie in her dog costume. Mum had made her a tail by cutting up an old pair of tights and stuffing one leg with more old tights, before sewing it onto her black leggings. She had been glad to find a job she could help with from her couch.

Mum helped me fix my hair in the *Alice in Wonderland* style Pauline wears it in the illustrations – held back with a wide ribbon. I got out the face paints and painted Maisie's face like a little black and white puppy. She looked really cute.

Zach and Bobby were already outside practising their lightsaber battle, and Dad was hanging up Maisie's birthday banner along the trellis at the back of the garden. Mum, still stuck on the couch but determined to help as much as she could, was blowing up one balloon after another. I tied them together in bunches and Maisie brought them out to the garden so Dad could hang them up too.

The doorbell rang – Ruby and Laura were here.

'Oh my God, oh my God, I'm so nervous!' Ruby gasped as soon as she saw me. She did look a bit pale. 'I keep thinking I'm going to forget my lines.'

I tried to reassure her. 'You'll be fine. We'll all help you out if you get stuck.'

The girls had brought everything they needed – Ruby had the character shoes and skirt she was going to wear for her solo dance, and Laura had her different costumes. She went up to my room to change into the first one while Ruby measured out the space on the patio for the fifteenth time, wanting to make sure she was finishing her solo in the centre. I looked at my watch, wondering where Meg was – it wasn't like her to be late.

I put out a row of cushions in front of the chairs, so the smaller children could sit there and get a good view. I also laid down a rug at one side of our 'stage' where cast members could sit when they weren't performing. I thought wistfully how great it would be to have a proper stage with curtains and lighting and backdrops, but when I stood back and took a look at how everything was coming together it actually looked pretty good.

Laura leaned out my bedroom window and called to me. 'Hannah, can you give me a hand with my hair? It keeps going wrong.'

I raced up the stairs to help. Laura's bun was slightly lopsided and small pieces were escaping on either side. 'We need more hair grips – millions of them – and tons of hairspray,' I told her.

I brought her into Mum and Dad's room so we could raid Mum's hair supplies. I was glad to have a bad hairdo to distract me from my nerves.

I didn't realise how long we had spent on Laura's hair until I heard a car pulling up outside and saw Maisie's friend Cormac get out, clutching a birthday present.

'Eeeek! It's party time!' I told Laura, shoving the last hair grip into place. 'We'd better go downstairs!'

The plan was to let the kids have a game of Pass the Parcel and a snack as soon as they arrived, then we'd bring them out to the garden and get the show underway. Dad would pass around some popcorn about halfway through in case they were getting restless. They were only five or six and even though we'd kept the show pretty short we didn't want it to get too much for their little attention spans.

More and more kids started arriving, and I was kept busy for a few minutes helping Dad to take their coats and bring them into the kitchen.

'That's right Ruth, sit down there beside Cormac – no Sally, we're going to have a snack in a few minutes – Bobby, can you show John where the toilet is?'

Ruby came into the kitchen, looking worried. 'Hannah, Meg's not here yet.'

'That's weird,' I said. 'Maybe she's forgotten the time – I'll pop over and get her.'

But just then the doorbell rang again, and I had to answer it. This time it was some of the neighbours Dad had invited to watch the show. I started feeling nervous all over again – it was bad enough making a fool out of myself in front of Maisie's friends, but all these grown-ups watching too was just too scary!

I was about to close the door behind them when I spotted the silver car outside Meg's house.

'Laura!' I hissed. 'Is that the car you were talking about?'

Laura and Ruby both came to the door.

'Yes, that's it!' Laura said. 'Now do you think it's just

someone selling house alarms?'

'No,' I admitted. 'I think you're right – there's something going on.'

'Should I call the police?'

'And say what, exactly?'

'I don't know,' Laura said.

'Let's go over there and see what's going on,' I said. 'Come on, we'll go around the back way.'

In the kitchen Dad had all the children playing Pass the Parcel and was sneakily stopping the music at a different child each time, so that each one got a chance to unwrap a layer. Zach was busy showing the neighbours to their seats, and Bobby was passing around cups of orange squash. Dad had helped Mum out to the garden so she could sit in a garden chair with her foot up on a stool, and she was making small talk with the grown-ups while jiggling Emma on her knee.

'Won't be a sec, Mum,' I told her. 'We're just seeing what's keeping Meg.'

Just then, over the noise of the party guests, I heard raised voices coming from next door.

Chapter Twenty-One

I glanced anxiously at my friends, but Laura walked on purposefully. 'Come on, we have to see what's going on.'

Peeping in at the kitchen window, Laura stopped and clutched my arm. 'That's him!'

'The house alarm guy?' I asked.

'Yes. I mean, no! Meg's dad, or whoever he is.'

I sneaked a look. There was a tall dark-haired man sitting at the kitchen table. Cordelia was walking around the kitchen waving her arms in the air, Meg was standing nearby with her arms folded and all three of them were talking over each other.

'Should we knock?' Ruby whispered.

Laura suddenly looked nervous too. 'I feel like we're interfering in a family row. If that's what it is.'

Next thing the door opened and we heard Meg say, 'Look, I'm going now! My friends are depending on me.'

'Meg, wait …'

'No, Dad! We can talk about this later, OK?'

Meg came storming out the door, then stopped dead

when she saw us.

'Hi,' I said nervously, feeling like we'd been caught spying. 'We thought we'd better come and find you – it's time for the show.'

'Is everything OK?' Laura asked.

'Not really,' Meg said. 'My dad just showed up, and now my parents are fighting again.'

Cordelia appeared behind Meg at the door. 'Meg, darling … Oh.' She too stopped dead when she saw us.

'We were just looking for Meg,' I started to explain again.

'Of course, darlings! Your show! Can we come and watch?'

'Yes, of course,' I said, though Meg looked pretty cross. 'Do you want to come through the hedge?'

'Thanks, Hannah darling. Doug, these are Meg's friends.'

We finally got a proper look at the mysterious dark-haired stranger as Cordelia ushered him out into the garden.

'Hello,' he said. 'I've been hearing all about this show and I can't wait to see it. Meg just can't keep away from performing!' He beamed all round at us, not looking at all like someone who was going to try to kidnap Meg in broad daylight. And Cordelia definitely wasn't scared – just pretty irritated.

Meg showed them the way and pointed out some empty

seats at the back. She was about to follow them through the hedge, but I stopped her.

'Meg, what's going on?' I asked. 'Is that really your dad?'

'Yes.' Meg looked embarrassed. 'I know you guys were wondering about why I didn't talk about him, but it's just that my parents have this kind of ... tempestuous relationship, I guess you'd call it.'

'Oh, Meg, you should have just told us,' Laura said. 'I mean, that's pretty common for separated couples.'

'Well, that's the thing. They're not technically separated,' Meg said. 'They're just sort of – living in different countries at the moment. Mum wanted me to have a break from – um – Dad's work stuff, so she decided we'd move here for a while, and of course Dad had to stay behind.'

I was trying to get my head around it. It sounded pretty complicated.

'What does your dad do, exactly?' Laura asked.

Meg checked to see that her parents had moved out of hearing. 'I'm not really supposed to say.'

My imagination started to run wild, but Laura was two steps ahead of me. 'Is he in the secret service? Or is he on the run from a criminal gang?'

Meg started laughing. 'No, nothing like that. He, um, works in films. They both do actually.'

'In FILMS?' we all exclaimed at once.

'Shhhh!' Meg said. 'I told you I'm not supposed to talk

about it.'

Suddenly everything started to fall into place. Everything Meg knew about acting – all her little sayings about bad dress rehearsals and the show must go on. Cordelia's dramatic personality. Sadie's amazing Aladdin's Cave attic.

Another thought struck me. 'Has this got something to do with why you didn't want to tell your mum about the show?'

'Sort of.' She hesitated. 'There's a bit more to it, but I can't tell you everything yet. Sorry. I'm not even supposed to have told you this much!'

'We won't tell anyone,' I promised.

'I'm kind of relieved, actually,' Ruby said. 'Laura thought your dad was trying to kidnap you. She was all set to call the police.'

'RUBY!' Laura had turned scarlet. 'I wasn't really going to call the police.' She glanced sideways at Meg. 'Sorry, Meg. I guess I let my imagination run wild.'

Luckily Meg saw the funny side. 'Oh my God – that's just like you, Laura! No, it's just all been a bit crazy. Mum was fed up of Hollywood, and ...'

'HOLLYWOOD!' All three of us were staring at her, open-mouthed.

'Yes, well, that's where we were last anyway ...' Meg trailed off.

'Are you four stars nearly ready?' Dad was standing at

the hedge shading his eyes from the sun. 'I've got a fairly demanding audience here who aren't going to stay quiet for much longer.'

'Aaaaaagh. This is it, guys!' I said to my friends. 'Time to go on stage – we can't keep them waiting. You'll have to tell us the rest later, Meg. OK, everyone got everything they need? Laura, I left your Nana stuff on the chair in the kitchen so you can change quickly.'

Ruby looked almost sick with nerves. 'Don't worry, Ruby, you'll be fine,' I said. 'Remember if you get stuck and forget your lines just make something up, OK?'

One by one we slipped through the hedge. My mind whirling, I stepped on to the patio, facing our audience. All Maisie's little friends were sitting on rugs at the front, while the adults sat behind them on chairs. Meg's parents were sitting beside Mum. I spotted Rebecca from the library at the back, and she gave me a friendly smile. I took a deep breath.

'Thank you so much for coming, everyone, and welcome to Maisie's party.' I smiled at my little sister, sitting expectantly with the rest of the cast as she waited for her turn to come on. 'I'm very proud to welcome you to the very first show by Star Club – and guests. Our first act will be a scene from *Ballet Shoes* by Noel Streatfeild, starring Laura Ryan as Madame Fidolia, Meg Howard as Petrova, Ruby Callaghan as Posy, and me, Hannah Kiely, as Pauline.

We hope you enjoy the show.'

I happened to glance up just then and saw Tracey watching us from her bedroom window. My stomach lurched, thinking she'd be getting ready to mock us, but I told myself to ignore her.

All of us were in the first scene from *Ballet Shoes*. We had decided that I would do a little introduction to each scene. I explained to the audience that in this scene the Fossil sisters were going to their new stage school for the first time and were waiting to meet Madame Fidolia. I knew even as I was speaking that I was going too fast. Then I spotted Sadie in the back row of the audience. Dad must have let her in while we were at Meg's. She was smiling and nodding at me in encouragement. I took a deep breath and tried to settle my nerves as we began the scene.

'Look at all these photos!' I said, as Ruby, Meg and I walked around the stage, pretending to examine photos on the walls. Suddenly I started to relax a little bit. I wasn't me at all – I was Pauline, and what I was nervous about wasn't the audience watching, it was the fact that I was going to meet Madame Fidolia.

'Being on stage wouldn't be so bad if I could dress up as a cat like these children,' Meg, as Petrova, said. 'Doesn't it look like fun?'

'I'd rather be a dancer,' Ruby said. 'I'd like to have flowers in my hair.'

Posy's big sisters immediately scoffed at this, and it gave me a thrill to hear lots of laughter from the audience as I said the line 'Imagine being so vain – how could anyone want to be one of those girls when you could be a cat!'

Laura swept onto the stage, her long skirts rustling. 'Welcome, my pupils,' she said, looking and sounding like a middle-aged Russian lady. 'I will make you all into beautiful dancers, no?'

Before I knew it, we'd reached the end of the scene, and Meg and I stepped off the stage. The next scene had just Laura and Ruby, as Madame Fidolia watched Posy dance. Ruby quickly stripped off the jumper and skirt she'd worn for the first scene – she had her leotard and tights on underneath. I waited until she was ready and then switched on the music. As she'd predicted, Ruby's nerves disappeared completely when she was dancing, and she looked completely in control.

I sneaked a look at the audience – they were totally engrossed. Some of Maisie's little friends seemed particularly taken with Ruby's dancing, swaying along to the music. But I didn't have too much time to watch them, as I needed to get the next scene organised.

'Bobby! Zach!' I whispered. 'You're up next.'

The boys grabbed their lightsabers and came to stand at the side of the stage. Bobby started going over his lines in a very loud whisper.

'Shhhh!' I said very quickly, just as Madame Fidolia frowned at him. I frowned back at Laura to remind her to stay in character.

'That was beautiful, Posy!' Laura exclaimed as Ruby finished her dance. The distraction had made her forget her accent for a minute and she spoke in her normal voice, but she picked it up again with her next line. 'Next term you will come only to my classes. I am convinced that one day the world will know of Posy Fossil's dancing.'

Ruby and Laura stepped down from the stage as the audience clapped loudly, and I waited for the applause to die down before introducing the boys. I sat back down, wondering if the change of pace from *Ballet Shoes* to *Star Wars* was going to work. One thing that hadn't needed much rehearsal was getting the boys into character, since they pretty much lived and breathed *Star Wars*.

I watched anxiously as they said their opening lines and launched into battle. The audience were loving it, and some of Maisie's friends started taking sides, cheering for either Bobby or Zach.

The final part of their scene had them jumping on top of the garden table to continue the fight. In the dress rehearsal Zach had been practising a dramatic somersault off the table as a finale, but he hadn't been able to pull it off, and we'd agreed he'd leave it out. Now though I suddenly realised, from the look of grim concentration on his face, that he had made up his mind to do it. I gripped Meg's arm anxiously. Zach leapt into the air and performed a perfect somersault, landing neatly on both feet. I heard a little gasp from Mum before the audience erupted into cheers. No one looked more surprised than Zach, who stood there in shock for a moment before a grin slowly spread across his face. He and Bobby bowed again and again, thrilled with the audience reaction.

Next up was Pauline's biggest scene – the necklace scene, as we called it. Ever since Sadie had helped me with my part, I'd been determined to do it as well as I possibly could.

Laura changed into her Nana costume, which meant exchanging Madame Fidolia's brightly coloured fringed shawl for a faded pink cardigan and putting on a pair of small round glasses. With very little time between scenes and no proper dressing rooms this was the best we could do for a costume change, and she still had the same long black skirt and hairstyle, but it was amazing how effective these small changes were. And Laura herself seemed to switch effortlessly from one role to the other, dropping Madame Fidolia's dramatic gestures and expressions for Nana's kind but no-nonsense style.

I got up to announce the scene, explaining to the audience that Pauline had been called for an audition and they were trying to figure out what she should wear. This is it,

I told myself. This is my chance to really bring Pauline to life.

'Miss Jay says I've got an audition tomorrow and need to wear my best frock,' I began. 'But I don't have one. That old velvet one is too worn.'

As I started speaking I was very conscious of people I knew watching me – Mum and Dad, Rebecca, Ruby's parents, and above all Sadie. But suddenly it was as if the audience just faded away, and I was Pauline, trying to make Nana see that I couldn't possibly go to an audition in ordinary clothes. And when Petrova came up with the plan to sell the necklaces, my sudden sense of hope that we'd found a solution felt very real.

It might have been my imagination, but the applause at the end of the scene seemed like the loudest yet. Sadie was beaming at me, and Mum looked very proud. The rush of adrenalin was like nothing I'd ever experienced before, and I knew there and then that I wanted more than anything to be an actress.

Maisie's song was next, and she didn't need anyone to remind her. She strode confidently onto the stage, completely forgetting to let me introduce her first. I sat back down. It was pretty clear Maisie needed no introduction.

'Raindrops on bones and chasing kittens!' Maisie began, wiggling her bottom to make her tail move. 'Yummy treats and chewing Dad's slippers!'

The song went on like that for quite a while, getting more and more bizarre. I saw some of the grown-ups shifting in their seats and shuffling their feet, but Maisie's friends were leaning forward eagerly and one or two were even trying to sing along. Dad had been right – this act was just right for the key audience!

Maisie finished at last, then started bowing over and over again, before starting to chase her tail like a real dog – something that definitely wasn't meant to be part of the act. Finally I had to go up on stage and gently but firmly escort her off, still waving to her fans.

Ruby did her solo dance next, the one she'd been practising for her exam, and it was her mum's turn to glow with pride. Then it was time for our final scene from *Ballet Shoes*, where Posy comes to tell her sisters that she wants to go away to train as a ballerina in Czechoslovakia. I was still on a high from the previous scene and Meg seemed in top form too, all our previous nerves forgotten. This was the scene where Ruby had the most lines and I knew she was afraid she was going to forget them, but Meg's suggestion about dancing her lines worked like magic. Ruby had fitted actions to particular lines, folding her hands in front of her at one bit and turning her feet out a certain way at another bit, so that her lines seemed to flow out as smoothly as the steps in one of her dance routines.

As soon as Petrova said her final line, 'I wonder if other

girls had to be one of us, which of us they'd choose to be?' all the grown-ups in the audience rose to their feet, clapping and cheering. Maisie's friends started cheering too, and we had to take one bow after another. I glanced up again and saw that Tracey was now looking distinctly jealous. I smiled to myself, but I knew this moment was too precious to waste on thinking about Tracey. Instead I held hands with Meg and Laura, while Laura gripped Ruby's hand on the other side, and we bowed again. We kept looking at each other and grinning, hardly able to believe our first show had gone off so well.

Two hours later we had said goodbye to all of Maisie's party guests. The last of the paper cups and popcorn wrappers had been cleared up, along with all the Pass the Parcel layers. Emma was napping, Bobby and Maisie were opening Maisie's presents and giving them marks out of ten, and Zach had disappeared upstairs. Mum and Dad had invited Meg's parents to stay for coffee, and all four were inside talking. The four members of Star Club had the garden to ourselves at last. Ruby and I were lying flat on our backs on a rug, exhausted. Laura had a mirror propped up in front of her and was taking all the grips out of her hair, and Meg was sitting in the grass making a daisy chain.

'So are you going to tell us the rest of the story then

Meg?' I asked her at last. 'Do you miss Hollywood?'

'No.' Meg sounded very definite. 'Hollywood isn't for me. And Mum hates it. She's really a stage actress, but she got a part in a film and we moved out there. Then Dad got some work there too as a director. He had done some TV work in Ireland and the UK before, and a chance came up for him to direct a film. But Mum didn't like film work – she much prefers acting in front of a live audience. She comes from a theatrical family, you see. Sadie was an actress – she still gets parts sometimes, actually – and Grandad was a classical Shakespearean actor. They both did lots of behind the scenes work too – you have to sometimes because there isn't always enough acting work.'

'So that's why Sadie has all that stuff in her attic!' I said. 'I did wonder why she had such a huge collection of clothes and random stuff.'

Meg looked embarrassed. 'I know. I'm sorry I didn't tell you the truth. I just knew if I started talking about it the family background would all come out, and Mum didn't want me to say anything. All of those costumes and props come from different productions Sadie and Grandad were involved in over the years.'

'So did your mum want to come back to Ireland to work in theatre again?' Laura asked.

'Actually she really just wanted to have an ordinary life for a while,' Meg said. 'Get a job in an office and be home every evening to make dinner! She started saying I needed a normal upbringing and that it wasn't good for me to be dragged from one place to another all the time and that the Hollywood lifestyle wasn't good for a twelve-year-old. But Dad was just starting to get regular work and he didn't want to move, so they kept rowing about it. Then after, well, other stuff happened, Mum just flipped and said that was it, she was taking me home to Carrickbeg to have a break from all the craziness.'

'And then the first thing you do is make friends with me and join a drama club,' I said, suddenly understanding just how Cordelia must have felt.

Meg laughed. 'I know. Now you know why Mum was so weird about it!'

I felt like I was watching Meg transform before my eyes as she told us more about her former life in the glitz and glamour of Hollywood. I still felt like she was holding something back, but it looked like we were going to have to wait to find out what that was.

I looked around at the scattered remains of our show – Ruby's ballet bag, the boys' lightsabers, Maisie's dog ears, a programme someone had left behind on a chair. 'I can't believe it's all over,' I said.

'I know! It feels like we've been building up to it for so long,' Ruby said. 'I can't believe I'm not going to be Posy any more.'

'I'm really going to miss Petrova,' Meg said sadly.

'I'm NOT going to miss Madame Fidolia's hair,' Laura said, removing the final hair grip and flinging it onto the grass.

I grinned at her. I'd used so much hairspray that her hair still stayed plastered back to her head in a sticky blob.

'There's only one thing for it,' I said suddenly, scrambling to my feet. 'We're going to have to start planning our next show!'